T0160831

Praise for
Antoine Volodine

"These wonderful stories fool around on the frontiers of the imagination. All musical dogs, woolly crabs, children, and other detectives of the not-yet-invented should own this book."
—Shelley Jackson

"His quirky and eccentric narrative achieves quite staggering and electric effects. . . . Dazzling in its epic proportions and imaginative scope."
—*The Nation*

"Volodine isn't afraid to tangle animate and inanimate spirits, or thwart expectations. He delights in breaking down our well-honed meters of what's supposed to happen."
—Margaret Wappler, *Believer*

"His textured portraits are convincing and well-rendered, and he has written the type of open-ended work that will capture the attention of lovers of lit crit as fiction."
—*Publishers Weekly*

"The ramifying narrative strands of Volodine's novels fascinate, but they are almost impossible to describe."
—*3:AM Magazine*

"*Minor Angels* has all the markings of a masterpiece: compression, resonance, and vision."
—Terese Svoboda, *Literary Review*

Antoine Volodine

Post-Exoticism
in Ten Lessons,
Lesson Eleven

Translated from the
French by J. T. Mahany

OPEN LETTER
LITERARY TRANSLATIONS FROM THE UNIVERSITY OF ROCHESTER

Library of Congress Cataloging-in-Publication Data:

Volodine, Antoine.
   [Post-exotisme en dix leçons, leçon onze. English]
   Post-exoticism in ten lessons, lesson eleven / by Antoine Volodine ;
translated from French by J. T. Mahany. — First Edition.
     pages cm.
   ISBN 978-1-940953-11-3 (pbk. : alk. paper) — ISBN 1-940953-11-1 (pbk. : alk. paper)
   I. Mahany, J. T., translator. II. Title.
   PQ2682.O436P6913 2015
   843'.914—dc23

2014039621

Cet ouvrage publié dans le cadre du programme d'aide à la publication bénéficie du soutien du Ministère des Affaires Etrangères et du Service Culturel de l'Ambassade de France représenté aux Etats-Unis.

[This work, published as part of a program of aid for publication, received support from the French Ministry of Foreign Affairs and the Cultural Service of the French Embassy in the United States.]

This project is supported in part by an award from the National Endowment for the Arts.

ART WORKS.
arts.gov

Open Letter is the University of Rochester's nonprofit, literary translation press: Lattimore Hall 411, Box 270082, Rochester, NY 14627

www.openletterbooks.org

Post-Exoticism
in Ten Lessons,
Lesson Eleven

Lutz Bassmann,
Ellen Dawkes,
Iakoub Khadjbakiro,
Elli Kronauer,
Erdogan Mayayo,
Yasar Tarchalski,
Ingrid Vogel,
&
Antoine Volodine

L utz Bassmann passed his final days as we all did, between life and death. A rotten odor stagnated in the cell, which did not come from its occupant, but from outside. The sewers in the city were fermenting, the docks in the harbor were emitting a rancid signal, the covered markets were stinking terribly, as they often did in the springtime when both the waters and the temperature began to rise. The mercury in the thermometers never fell below 34° or 35° Celsius, and it always rose back up from its nightly drop to give way to oppressive grayness. Puddles of mold spread across every wall. In the hours preceding dawn, darkness grew in power in the depths of lungs, under the bed, under the nails. Clouds burst into cataracts under the slightest pretext. The noise of the storm haunted everyone. Ever since Bassmann began to feel unwell, the rain had not ceased its patter against the prison's façade, furnishing the silence with the sound of lead. It streamed over the exterior, crossed over the edge of the window, and gloomily drew lines of rust beneath the bars, onto the bulletin board that certain guards had baptized the "union board" and which resembled a very old cubist or futurist collage, very dense, very faded. The water zigzagged between the photographs and the newspaper clippings that Bassmann had pinned there, and which helped support him in his stay in the high-security sector, among us: this immobile voyage had already lasted for twenty-seven years, twenty-seven long, long, longer-than-long years. Then, the already-dirty liquid met up with a thin blackish ribbon wending its way to the bottom of the wall, thus mixing with the infiltrations from a leak in the plumbing, perhaps in the toilet's outflow pipe. No doubt there, yes, in this pipe, or in a pipe of the same kind. Over several months, the humidity had pierced the cement, which gradually expanded. Thus, when atmospheric pressure dropped, the stench rose. Hence these waves that heavily velveted the surroundings, similar to the vapors of a cadaver on the march toward the nothing. The administration was waiting for Bassmann's death before undertaking any renovations. The guards had made this known to the prisoner with the obtuse frankness common to horrid bipeds, and without snickering, for in their impatience to see the end of history they did not even snicker anymore in front of him when they spoke of his end. Bassmann himself was not waiting for anything. He faced our damaged portraits and sat there watching them. He contemplated the spongy, almost-illegible photographs, the obsolete portraits of his friends, men and women, all dead, and he looked back on who knows what trouble and, at the same time, the fact that he had lived marvelously in their company, when they were all free and shining, the time when all of us, from the first to the last, were something other than. But that's not important. I have said "our" faces, among "us," all of "us." This is a process of the literary lie, but one which, here, plays with a truth hidden upstream of the text, with a not-lie inserted into the real reality, elsewhere rather than in fiction. Let us say, in order to simplify, that Lutz Bassmann was our spokesperson to the end, both his and that of everyone and everything. There have been several spokespeople: Lutz Bassmann, Maria Schrag, Julio Sternhagen, Anita Negrini, Irina Kobayashi, Rita Hoo, Iakoub Khadjbakiro, Antoine Volodine, Lilith Schwak, Ingrid Vogel. This list contains deliberate errors and is incomplete. It follows the post-exoticist principle according to which a portion of shadow always subsists in the moment of explanation or confession, modifying the confession to the point of rendering it unusable to the enemy. To objective appearances, the list is only a sarcastic way of telling the enemy one more time that they will learn nothing. For the enemy is always part stalker, disguised and vigilant among readers. We must continue to speak in a way that denies the enemy any profit. We must do this even as we testify before a tribunal whose authority we do not recognize. We devise a solemn proclamation, in a language that appears to be the same as that of the judges, but it is one that the judges listen to with dismay or boredom, as they are incapable of making sense of it . . . We recite it for ourselves and for men and women not present . . . Our remarks coordinating in no circumvention of phrase with the magistrates' understanding . . . There was nothing extraordinary about the rain that sounded and rang out in Bassmann's agony during this period; it was completely expected in the month of April. In this region, touched by the tail end of the monsoons, we were in the habit of associating springtime not with green rebirth as is the tradition in occidental literature, but with the slow and loud din of the deluge, mugginess, and mephitic atmospheres. Inside the prison, pestilences alter in intensity by the second as they circulate in an unpredictable manner that prevents any immunization. A feeling of suffocation tormented us from dawn-to-dawn. It is not surprising to discover that psychosomatic illnesses spring up during this phase of the prison calendar. Added to the respiratory troubles are the troubles of solitude. It was extremely difficult for us to converse between cells, on account of all the background noise, from the monotonous sweeping and the trickling that kept on at every hour, muddying the content of our messages. That year, the "we" was, even more than normally, a literary lie, as much a convention of fiction as Lutz Bassmann was alone. Now he was alone. He had reached the moment of our common adventure that several of us had described, in books completed or otherwise, as that of ultimate defeat. When the last surviving member on the list of the dead—and, this time, it was Bassmann—stammered his final syllable, then, on this side of the story as well as beyond it, only the enemy would keep strutting straight ahead, undefeated, invincible, and, among the victims of the enemy, no spokesperson would now dare come to interpret or reinterpret any of our voices, or to love us. Lucid despite the split personalities corrupting his agony, Bassmann sought only to communicate with the deceased. He no longer tapped on the washbasin pipes or on the door, saying, for example, "Calling cell 546," or on the sealed siphon behind the

1. Fragmentary Inventory of Deceased Dissidents

Arostegui, Maria (1975)*
Bach, Matthias (1991)
Bartok, Giovan (1991)
Bassmann, Lutz (1990)
Bedobul, Kynthia (1988)
Breughel, Anton (1975)
Breughel, Istvan (1985)
Campanini, Giuseppe (1988)
Clementi, Maria (1975)
Damtew, Oleg (1998)
Dawkes, Ellen (1990)
Domrowski, Monika (1998)
Draeger, Manuela (2001)
Echenguyen, Irena (1981)
Echenguyen, Maria (1976)
Fincke, Elia (1998)
Garcia Muñoz, Maria (1985)
Gardel, Wolfgang (1975)
Gompo, Khrili (1980)
Heier, Barbara (1991)
Henkel, Maria (1980)
Hinz, Mario (1998)
Hoo, Rita (1992)

---

* Year in parentheses indicates date of incarceration at high-security sector.

Iguacel, Maria (1975)

Khadjbakiro, Iakoub (1977)

Khorassan, Jean (1996)

Kim, Petra (1992)

Kobayashi, Irina (1991)

Koenig, Astrid (1990)

Kronauer, Elli (1999)

Kwoll, Maria (1975)

Lethbridge, William (1992)

Lukaszczyk, Vassilissa (1987)

Malaysi, Jean (1979)

Malter, Hugo (1990)

Marachvili, Türkan (1992)

Marconi, Ivo (1992)

Mayayo, Erdogan (1998)

Nachtigall, Roman (2000)

Negrini, Anita (1977)

Nordstrand, Verena (1986)

Ossorguina, Raïa (1986)

Ostiategui, Leonor (1996)

Ostiategui, Pablo (1996)

Peek, Marina (1998)

Petrokian, Aram (1992)

Pizarro, Hans-Jürgen (1998)

Reddecliff, Dimitri (1990)

Retsch, Dorothea (1975)

Retzmayer, Rita (1979)

Retzmayer, Zeev (1976)

Samarkande, Maria (1978)

Santander, Monika (1982)

Sauerbaum, Maria (1996)

Schnittke, Maria (1980)

Schrag, Maria (1975)

Schwack, Lilith (1979)

Sherrad, Aidan (1990)

Soledad, Irena (1977)

Soudayeva, Maria (1975)

Sternhagen, Julio (1975)

Tarchalski, Yasar (1990)

Thielmann, Maria Gabriella (1992)

Thielmann, Ralf (1982)

Velazquez, Sonia (2000)

Vlassenko, Jean (1987)

Wallinger, John (1991)

Weingand, Anita (1986)

Wernieri (1975)

Wolff, Rebecca (2001)

Wolguelam, Jean (1975)

Zhang, Yann (1977)

toilet bowl, asking for cell 1157, or on the bars of the window, saying "Bassmann here . . . please respond . . . Bassmann is listening . . . please respond . . ." Now he knocked nowhere. He concentrated his gaze on us, the photographs of those who had preceded him in disappearing, and he made the smallest of murmurs pass through his lips, pretending not to be dead and reproducing a whispering technique that the most tantric among us had many a time used in their romånces: with an audible exhalation, the narrator prolongs, not his or her own existence, but the existence of those who are going to dwindle into nothing, whose memory can only be preserved by the narrator. Word by word, moan after moan, Lutz Bassmann struggled to make last the mental edifice that would eventually become dust once again. His breath merged with the putrid sewers that wandered through the prison. He still tenuously held on to reality and he managed to keep together fragments. He managed to keep his voice from giving out again. So that for one hour more, two and a half hours, one more night, the worlds that we had built with swift carpentry and defended would persist. Mental edifice . . . Worlds . . . Swift carpentry . . . What is . . . Huh? I will respond. That is what we had called post-exoticism. It was a construction connected to revolutionary shamanism and literature, literature that was either written by hand or learned by heart and recited, as the administration through the years would sometimes forbid us any paper material; it was an interior construction, a withdrawal, a secret welcoming land, but also something offensive that participated in the plot of certain unarmed individuals against the capitalist world and its countless ignominies. This fight was now confined solely to Bassmann's lips. It was suspended in a breath. As thirty years of incarceration had left his mind feeble, and reduced his creative spirit to scraps, his final murmurs no longer obeyed the logics of pioneers, combatants, oneiric footprints, or enthusiasm, without which the post-exoticist project had produced no more than two or three works. During his death throes, Lutz Bassmann's only wish was to stir the embers that he had guarded, and not be absorbed too quickly along with them by the nothingness. But even before, at the beginning of the ten years, maybe because he estimated that the confidants were already unattainable or no longer existed, it seemed that he had lost his creative spark. His latest works, his final romanesque jolts, took shelter under rather unattractive and uninspired titles, such as *To Know How to Rot, To Know How Not to Rot*, or *Structure of Deconstructed Obscurity*, or *Walk Through Childhood*. These are narrative poems and Shaggås, supposedly compact pieces diluted into vast *arrière-garde* logorrheas that one can take no pleasure in reading. There are also romånces, such as *About-Face Vandals, One Thousand Nine Hundred Seventy-Seven Years Before the World Revolution*, and even *The Mantis*, but the brooding that inspired them has devolved into nothing communicable. Their encryption is vain, their undeniable beauty is vain, maybe simply because no one—no one is listening. No living being other than Lutz Bassmann is paying attention. In such works, the idea of connivance with the reader, so oily and so generously spread onto the clockwork of official literature, has been disregarded to even the smallest details. Here we have the terminal rumblings, the ultimate punctuated throaty rasps of post-exoticism . . . POST-EXOTICISM. That word again. Here again this heavy term. Around it we have circled, from the beginning, like vultures around a carcass. WHAT IS POST-EXOTICISM? An insolent question, very unwelcome on the day of Bassmann's death, but its appearance here demonstrates that a half-century after *Minor Angels*, by Maria Clementi, sympathizers, on the outside, have not . . . Demonstrates that the incarcerated have been left alone. A symposium on post-exoticism was organized with Lutz Bassmann's involvement before the '00s of the twenty-first century, eighteen or nineteen years ago. It lived more or less in 1997. Beyond the walls of the prison, this must have been an age of hollow editorials, or of reflux toward what official literature itself considered the worst. Two popular chroniclers had been sent to us by a cultural magazine in general circulation, subsidized, I believe, by mafia industrialists in meat and construction. I say "I," and "I believe," but this is again just a matter of pure convention. The first-person singular serves to accompany the voice of others, it signifies nothing more. Without damage to the understanding of this poem, one can consider that I have been dead for ages, and not take the "I" into account . . . For a post-exotic narrator, anyway, there is not the thickness of a piece of cigarette paper between the first-person and others, and hardly any difference between life and death. But let us classify the problems. I spoke of two salaried employees of the dominant ideology, two virtuosos of journalism, of the star system and writing, a man and a woman who, for the occasion, had muted their mercantile convictions and come before us wearing the faded finery of intellectuals neither spineless, nor completely orthodox. They wanted, they announced, to inquire about prison literature, and shine a new and favorable light on românces, several volumes of which had appeared outside of the prison, under the signature of one of our figureheads. I also think that General Intelligence desired to evaluate the state of our forces and to form an opinion on the persistence or extinction of our capability to harm, on the chances of the survival of egalitarian propaganda in the new millennium. The journalists presented themselves by insisting on their capacity as novelists sometimes at odds with the authorities, as, like in all totalitarian societies, those who are approved by the censor are also those who have the right to express themselves officially against the censor, and they articulated their authorial names with a casual humility, hoping maybe to impress us with their notoriety, with the value that credit agencies and the public recognize, but, as we were indifferent to this kind of authority, and as their magazine had never inspired anything in us but contempt, they still appeared as they were in both reality and in the world of media: two mercenaries of speech, Niouki and Blotno, Niouki the woman, Blotno the man, capable of theorizing on art and philosophizing on the fate of the people, capable over several hours of adapting themselves to our vision of the world, of entering into a dialogue with us, and even of getting friendly with us, capable of everything. They had five or six afternoons; they worked with us in turns, according to a program that we thwarted as quickly as possible. Anonymous, imperturbable, silent, a police officer attended the sessions and recorded us on a tape recorder. We were summoned to the interview room one after the other. The Blotno faced us with a notebook and pen, no doubt because he had been informed that only the police would be allowed to listen to the taped recording. As he was constantly scribbling, he hardly ever lifted his eyes in our direction, eyes that shone with a relative absence of insincerity, very blue, a myopic, almost Prussian blue. If I stray from the striking color of his irises, I now feel powerless to describe his physical attributes, the particularities of his head. In a pinch, I believe I could remember his corpulence. He was about medium-sized. The Niouki is less

2. Maria Clementi's "Minor Angels," romånce, 1977

Moyocoatzin and Mlatelpopec, two beings with the appearance of grotesque birds, on the whole semi-human, rid themselves of the sorrow of reclusion or exile inside an eternally burning shopping mall. Their daily life unfolds uneventfully and without contact with the outside world. They do not regret the past and they do not speak, whereby the reasons and the circumstances of their punishment remain in the shadows. As they are gifted with the power to stagnate time both in and around themselves, Moyocoatzin and Mlatelpopec adapt to living in the flames, since the burning is constantly pushed back later and later. They live among the beauty of the fire and its incessant roaring for a paradoxical duration of time: a second can take a century to elapse from beginning to end. The action in the romånce develops on this principle, in which the infinitely brief overlaps or sits next to eternity, and even distends it.

The pair settled near the record department, and occasionally listened to music. Having been condemned to perpetuity, they know that they will never escape from this howling place. They do not get bored. They listen to operas deformed by the heat, they tell each other anecdotes, and, as they do not have any books at their disposal, they invent some. They imagine an exterior reality and they comment on it. Bivouacking amid the smoke, sometimes they sleep, then they compare their dreams.

Suddenly, the telephone rings. Someone wishes to join them. It is Gardel, a revolutionary who is calling from his cell, where he is in the middle of immolating himself, and who, on this occasion, has discovered *flambulence*: the displacement of the self within fire, the petrification of time, the migration from one body to another.

We are witness to Moyocoatzin and Mlatelpopec's distress. For those who have habituated themselves to a routine existence, the arrival of a mutineer can be very bothersome. They do not want their music store to become a center for international subversion, the calls for revolt carried on the voices of the singers who they adore. Little by little carried away with pettiness, they conceive of a hostile welcome for the visitor, a path filled with traps.

But the interloper penetrates the flames in an invulnerable form. Instead of taking a natural path, he walks through the interior of his hosts' dreams, thus learning their secrets along the way. He now too possesses the form of a minor angel, a large fireproof bird. And when Moyocoyatzin and Mlatelpopec move to destroy him, he defends himself.

Of course, like in every romånce, a formalist dimension has been added to the romanesque intrigue. It passes unperceived in the reading, but it exists. The final version of this manuscript is exactly 66,666 (sixty-six thousand six hundred sixty-six) words long.

nonexistent in my memory. Her chest seemed to me like that of a cow or a cowgirl. Her breasts made an impression on me, but I don't remember exactly what that impression was. For that matter, they weren't of any interest to—Lutz Bassmann went first and kept his mouth shut the whole time. In order to break the drawn-out silence, the Niouki summarized the stages that, according to her, post-exoticism had passed through since *Minor Angels*, Maria Clementi's first romånce, written in 1977. Several generations have followed, continued the Niouki, founded by the same implacable ideology of radical egalitarianism. But these generations have reflected, she said, moments of difference, fractures with contemporary history that have widened with time. As soon as she pronounced the "u" in "fractures," a gust of rank air blew in under the door, from the monitoring room, and surrounded us, her, the recorder, and me. I remember the composition of this bouquet: wet cardboard, sewer rat, mosses found in public urinals (certainly from those at the top of the avenue), rotten seafood, laundry from the communal district, rust, sludge, scrap iron, vegetable soup, fritters. I analyzed and enumerated all of them, pretending to be sullenly meditating. I regret that I no longer know if, at the time, the shape of the journalist's breasts displeased or charmed me, and if the other prisoners beheld her with rapacity or boredom, based on what they guessed of her body through the grille and through her clothing. The memory of our reactions would have added a bit of life to this hammered-out, heavy-voiced exposé, as if the Niouki were addressing a studious and humorless audience. The first generation included historical figures from the guerilla, discoursed the Niouki, those who hadn't died with guns in hand and who one day had believed that the proletarian torrents would unfold in the capitals . . . that the poorest of the people would rally in incendiary utopias and triumph . . . and that they would put them into action around the globe . . . Maria Iguacel, Maria Arostegui, Julio Sternhagen, Maria Clementi, Maria Echenguyen, Irena Echenguyen, Maria Schrag, Wernieri, Maria Soudayeva, Wolfgang Gardel, Iakoub Khadjbakiro, to cite only some, had hoped for that . . . Once incarcerated, this vanquished army, this hard kernel of egalitarianism, discharged its unfaded passion under romanesque form . . . under disheveled form, under sumptuous, fantastical, exuberant forms, under thunderous form. It is evident that the Niouki, bogged down in the fact that she has always written in the aesthetic of the best sellers, was not speaking in these terms, but I recall that she tried to cheer Bassmann up by flattering him, evoking our names with grandiloquence. I also noticed that she avoided treating us like murderers or monsters. It was a period, she elaborated, when hope of global upheaval always vibrated somewhere on the surfaces of your texts. Correct, Niouki, I thought, the cornerstones of post-exotic literature were developed during the sixties . . . during those years when, in spite of defeat, the possibility of revival still remained . . . Years of underground hope, luminous despite the lead and despite the violence of the prisons, I told myself. While the Niouki's didactic discourse spread, Lutz Bassman hadn't opened his mouth at all. The Niouki swelled her mammal flesh to epic proportions, and she shook, reciting a speech she had doubtless already given on a talk show or at a conference in front of an audience of policemen and academics. The calendar indicated a springtime date, let's say April, let's say April thirteenth since false

---

precisions are indispensable, since the act of speaking requires one to lie, then to rummage through minutia in one's lies. April thirteenth or fourteenth. The rain beat against the walls of the prison, as it would during the days preceding Lutz Bassmann's death, in that spring to which I have already alluded. Some streams bubbled on the outside, the damp spread, all the objects in the room looked like they had been coated in glue. The sewer odor dispersed, little by little. Bassmann sniffed. His eyes were open, but he wasn't listening. He fixed his gaze not on the face of the journalist, nor on her breasts, but on the grille that divided the room in two. The iron stank less than in the rooms of the ordinary condemned, with the common criminals, as, on account of the political prisoners' isolation, it rarely received their spit, their snot. Rarely, if ever. Visitors were permitted, in theory, but none ever came. Our contacts and allies had disappeared, our advocates had been mutilated or killed, one after the other. But let's be brief. On the surface of your texts, the Niouki repeated while readjusting her bra. The rain grew in intensity. A hand moved and polished something on the tape recorder. No matter which mammary the Niouki emphasized, the police officer remained stony, only interested in the optimal quality of the sound. The Shaggå, the romånce, the interjoists, the fantasia, continued the Niouki, nodding, and the sub-genres such as the recitact, the lesson, and the narract, are present from the first lyric manifestations by the first-generation writers. And the murmuract? I thought. That fat cow forgot the murmuract. And we were wondering, Blotno and I, said the Niouki. Is this not an extraordinary phenomenon? You make up new literary genres that don't seem experimental at all; instead they seem viable, and like they won't

3. The Shaggå

A debate both playful and erudite has always surrounded the question of the origins of the Shaggå. Several authors' names occur in concurrence from which it must be determined who invented the form and who, subsequently, immediately afterward, materialized its beauty. This competition has no concrete base; its motive can be found neither in susceptibilities, nor acts of disloyalty. It is, quite simply, one of the poetic artifices by which the genre expresses its very, very great particularity.

The very first collection of Shaggås is signed Infernus Iohannes, the pseudonym behind which dozens of creators or post-exoticist collectives could have concealed themselves. Its title is *Mirrors of the Cadaver*; it came to light in 1979. Not much later, *Myriam's Silence* by Jean Wolguelam (1979) and *The Cold Princes* by Maria Echenguyen (1980) appeared.

These three works established the rules of the genre, without which it would have spent much time groping about for a sense of itself. From its birth, the Shaggå has reached an unsurpassable level of perfection, a maturity that does not suffer from childish illness. *Mirrors of the Cadaver* is not an experimental prototype, but a work that belongs to the domain of post-exoticist academism. The authors who, as a result, have chosen the Shaggå as a mode of expression have not felt the need to alter any of its characteristics. To the contrary, they have imitated the canonical models, introducing no variants besides the inoffensive, under no pretext do they diverge from the path, ever vigilant to avoid betraying Infernus Iohannes.

A Shaggå always breaks down into two distinct textual masses: one part, a series of *seven sequences* rigorously identical in length and tone; the other, a *commentary*, in which the style and dimensions are free.

The sequences illustrate a lyrical anecdote that one may guess to be extracted from a complex and lush mythological world, of which one must oneself deduce and imagine the fundamental elements, as nothing of the sort is explained fully in the text. Seven facets of the same event are described; the action obeys at the same time principles of uncertainty and a stubborn demand for narrative stagnation, even repetition. One begins to doubt what is happening, and though only a single event is taking place, it must be witnessed multiple times. A finely worked and highly valued sentence structure, a rich vocabulary, and an ornamental prose uphold it all.

The obtained effect has implications that go beyond the aesthetic. It is in relation with the status of the reader, of the listener. The Shaggå seems to address a reader who is in close ideological and cultural connivance with the author, but it plays before a vast, unknown audience, among which unfriendly entities are dissimulated. This is why the text delivers no significant message. The only thing communicated is the form of the message it could have taken if it had been transmitted and encrypted. The classic Shaggå offers to the detained reader—its only real addressee—a time of unfinished complicity. To the occasional reader, it offers a moment of calm poetic caress. To the rapacious reader, an ambiguous space where his or her hostility is squandered.

The commentary, opposite the seven sequences, is a discourse not governed by imperatives of style. However, its impulses and its orientation show that it does not disrupt the aesthetic of mistrust that governs in-depth the mechanism of the sequences. One might say that the substance of the questionings and debates is a throwback to the xenophilosophy as little divulged as the xenomythology discussed above.

The temporal paradoxes, the themes of illusion and incertitude frequently occupy the first level of the commentary; it is common, at the same time, to wonder about the identity of the author or authors of the Shaggå rather than the characters read about in the sequences. Some keys are supplied, which explain nothing, or suggest that certain truths exist, essential, monstrously abused and hidden, elsewhere, rather than in the text and the fallacious reality that the texts explore. These suggestions always have a filigreed character, designed to connect the unconscious with the conscious.

The Shaggås of Infernus Iohannes are often cited in the literature of the high-security sector and, in several cases, are completely reappropriated and inserted into romånces. Vassilissa Lukaszczyk, for example, utilizes this borrowing technique in her writing of *Lisbon, Last Edge*. It is agreed that this is not a form of plagiarism, as the basest literatures

---

have accustomed us to read, but that which, in the critical vocabulary of post-exoticism, we call an *homage*: a reincarnation in a fraternal literary body, the possibility of a new journey in a new book.

The original manuscript of the collection *Mirrors of the Cadaver* remained for some time with Maria Schrag, in cell 559, but was destroyed when the cell's occupant committed suicide by fire. It included an introduction in a cryptic language and three Shaggås, the titles of which follow:

—*Shaggå of Ayarirpu*

—*Shaggå of the Marble Witnesses*

—*Shaggå of the Return of Abdallah, Captain of the Sword's Roar*

While we render homage to Infernus Iohannes, we think with friendship and love of Maria Schrag, Vassilissa Lukaszczyk, Jean Wolguelam, Maria Echenguyen, and all of our companions.

INGRID VOGEL

change afterward, except for in the details. Isn't this curious? Yes, said Ellen Dawkes, indeed. The rain beat against the prison; pushed by gusts of wind, it volleyed the enormous walls, the glass roof, as if it wanted to ravage them, or like heroic commandos who would never come, launching suicidal assaults to liberate the detainees. Ellen Dawkes replaced Lutz Bassmann, who had been uncooperative. She resembled a resident of a psychiatric asylum, one of those touching madwomen who one sees so often wandering in our post-exotic works. She was sitting on the stool bolted into the concrete, she put her two elbows on the bar destined to receive her elbows or her hands, and, disheveled, rumpled, ugly, she did not give the impression of ever having been a great criminal, even though she had riddled the bodies of a dozen higher-ups responsible for the evils of the world with bullets, the idea of repenting not crossing her mind for a second. From life to death between her hands had passed the rich of poor countries and the rich of rich countries, traffickers in human flesh, proprietors of empires. Personally, I do not see why she, or I, should have shown any remorse. And you? But let's return to this discussion, to the sticky visitor's room, to the sound of the rain. Ellen Dawkes emitted a pensive murmur, so soft that the policeman and the journalist had to incline their heads at similar angles, in the same contortion as frustrated auditors. The Shaggå, yes, mumbled Ellen Dawkes. Seven sequences of equal length . . . The uncertainty of things . . . The illusory . . . The extreme beauty of untransmitted messages . . . The splendor of non-unobscured mythologies . . . Talk about that, if you wish, the Niouki requested. Since we're on the subject. You yourself have written a collection of Shaggås: *The Death One Crosses Before Love.* A very tragic piece, very classic, I think. "Deaths," corrected Ellen Dawkes, in a clearer voice, then, without waiting for the journalist's excuses, she returned to her whispering. *The Deaths One Crosses* . . . In any case, I have nothing to say to you . . . We don't share a critical language . . . The hyperclassicism of the Shaggå does not coincide with any of the norms of your academism . . . Shaggås can only be decoded through values and experiences that your literature has never recognized as its own . . .

I say "your" academism, "your" literature, but . . . Do not look for
any elegance here . . . some kind of paradoxical footbridge fated to
stretch between you and us . . . lady . . . You know, the chasm that
separates us cannot be crossed . . . Your literature and ours . . .
don't speak to each other . . . Through intellectual laziness, you
believe post-exoticism to be one aesthetic among many, a bizarre
variant on magical post-modernism . . . even though post-exoticism is to your literature what . . . Her voice broke, returned, the
bits of phrases overlapping, she made no effort to talk over the
storm. The Niouki strained to hear as she scribbled. She tran-
scribed. She succeeded in transcribing this miniscule stream. Nothing has been awoken by the Shaggås of the first generation . . .
Ellen Dawkes rasped, and she stood. Her voice had again dwindled
in intensity, though now there was a terrible violence to it, terrible
and bitter. Now, she was standing facing the grille, fixing her eyes
neither on the Niouki nor on her shadow. The tape recorder's elec-
tronic membranes hardly registered more than the sound of lips
moving, but it was evident that Ellen Dawkes was screaming. No
fire! . . . in whatever realm that! . . . she cried, like in a silent film
when a witch curses an arrogant civilization. The others of this
founding prose are dead, executed in their cells! . . . Hanged! . . .
Strangled high up! . . . With belts that had been confiscated years
before! . . . the day they came here! . . . and which by a miracle!
. . . Or suicide by jerry can! . . . or with a hunting knife! . . . even
though the only utensils! . . . we're allowed! . . . are! . . . a spoon
and a comb! . . . The Niouki had recoiled slightly and she was
there, behind the lattice, frightened by this outpouring of silence.
Her famous journalist hands trembled, her successful author's

chest was riled, her breasts looked appalled, pointless. It was hot and humid, I've already said that. Everyone was soaked with sweat. These texts have circulated under difficult conditions, declared Yasar Tarchalski, once Ellen Dawkes had been escorted back to the fourth floor, cell 1372. The interview began again after a day of interruption. The prison guards had put away their clubs, the audience had seized control once more, the police officer was reinstated in front of his tape recorder, the orator answered questions, the deluge denoted a pause. The gutters were heard jingling, the city snorting behind the barbed wire dotting the tops and sides of the outer walls. A bird made a solitary call, two held notes, strong and spectacularly harmonious. Wait, said Tarchalski. You know that bird? It sang like that years ago, around this time. From April to June. Then, it disappeared. Tarchalski imitated the bird. You don't know what kind of bird it is? he insisted. I heard that cry for the first time in a forest in Sarawak, Malaysia, in the time when I walked freely and when there were forests, a cry that you can't confuse with any other, and I supposed it came from a woodsy, equatorial species, but no, eventually, seeing that. He whistled again. No, said the Blotno, who had replaced the Niouki. In the past, I knew how to identify certain caws, but that one, no. In turn, he mimicked the bird. No, that means nothing to me, he said. That's not a caw, said Yasar Tarchalski. The policeman leaned over the tape recorder. His impassibility had reached a crisis. He shrugged. Ornithology infuriated him and he couldn't hide it. We need to talk about your sympathy for birds, for all animals, said the Blotno. It's an important theme in post-exoticism. The speeches to animals, the animality of many characters, fraternization with birds and even insects. It's important, right? . . . But let's save that for later. I would first like to come back to the question of formalism. The authors of the high-security sector, from the seventies onward, have explored half a dozen new forms. From their first texts. Why such a frenzy? Oh, said Tarchalski, they foresaw the horror of being forever imprisoned, they organized themselves for future function. With frenzy they circumscribed the territories of their interior freedom, which were found to correspond to the territories of their own literature. There were subjects held close to their hearts, anecdotes where they felt their exile would be softer, and, at the same time, they sought to define literary supports that wouldn't agree with you, and that wouldn't reproduce any of your traditions, or any of your official conformities or anticonformities. They invented empty forms that you never had the occasion to pollute, and they filled them with visions foreign to your sensibilities. Thereby they also came into dissent. They invented the romånce genre so as not to be involved with you or your attempts at renovating the novel, with all the mercantile jugglings of the institutional avant-gardes. It's a process of aversion, get it? Aversion and malevolence. They attached their works to new categories, romånce, Shaggås, etc., first and foremost to affirm that despite your saber-rattling, you were still the representatives and loquacious dogs of the enemy, the enemy's entertainers, lyricists for a world meant to be destroyed. Do I make myself clear, Blotno? . . . You still want me to vary my terms? . . . The rain, without warning and without frailty, began falling again. Enormous sooty clouds burst above us, and in the visiting room, once again, a hot vapor swirled, whose transparent and somewhat-drooling texture

4. The Romånce

The romånce belongs to the family of romanesque forms, and its narrative ambition, its width, its style, bring it close to the novel. Nevertheless, it is distinguished by several traits that will be exposed here in summary fashion.

1. Unity of Blood

Despite the great diversity of subjects broached, and even if the characters and decors change considerably according to the authors, one cannot read a romånce without getting the impression that it shares a kinship with other romånces that precede or follow it. This impression sometimes remains hazy, but it is founded: bloodlines exist between all works of the genre.

Something unifying always ends by appearing on one reading level or another: a thematic of extremist despair, an aggressive principle bound to the extreme, in hypotheses of no return, all sustained by visions, ruminations, and a memory whose darkness could not have crystallized anywhere else but here, in the high-security sector. Each anecdote follows its own independent route, not caring whether or not it resonates in harmony with the rest of the penal production, but, in a direct or indirect way, what is said in romånces always comes back to a collectivity of prisoners and the prison.

2. Non-Repentance of the Narrator

The narrator tells the story and is not always invested in a conjured theatrical role. However, when his or her ideology is mentioned—no matter whom the characters and whatever their political conscience and what becomes of them in the fiction—that ideology is one of criminal egalitarianism, fanatical, unrepentant and unvanquished, and it returns, in turn, to prison.

3. Death of the Narrator

The narrator is preoccupied with his relation to the literary lie. He finds himself in conflict with the narration, in part because fiction often leads him to espouse a strictly tragic destiny, but also because the very idea of narration, not at all effective at metamorphosing the real, repulses him.

This is why, seduced more by mutism or autistic rumination than by the romanesque, the narrator seeks to disappear. He hides himself, he appoints his function and his voice to strawmen, to heteronyms that will exist in his place. A straw writer signs the románces, a straw narrator orchestrates the fiction and is integrated as such. In the high-security sector, custom dictates that heteronyms take the identity of a recently deceased detainee, either by murder or suicide.

Thus, a characteristic of the románce is vocal distortion and the confusion in the actual name of the givers and takers of speech. Behind the book's author, spokesperson, and signatory, and behind the voice of the narrator or narrators staged in the book, one must replace an *overnarrator* who voluntarily erases himself and who, in a process of intimate camaraderie, forces his voice and thought to reproduce the melodic contour of a disappeared voice and thought. Thus comes this insistence of the narrator to pretend he is already dead: perhaps this is the sole literary lie onto which he can hold without unease.

4. Non-Opposition of Opposites

The dynamic of the romånce is articulated in a way that could not be inscribed in a traditional romanesque universe, as it rests entirely on a conception of opposites where opposites merge.

The victim is executioner, the past is present, the achievement of action is its beginning, stillness is movement, the author is a character, the dream is reality, the unliving is living, silence is speech, etc.: antagonisms are clearly defined, but inside an oscillating or looping intellectual system, which modifies the nature of oppositions and, in a nutshell, attributes to them no importance.

On this question, the will of authorial dissent is total, and, concretely, it is affirmed in refusing to give justifications or to lead a polemic against the "good sense" of the adversary. The logic of non-opposition of opposites has always marked post-exotic thought. It feels sufficiently strong and totalitarian as to have no need to explain its singularity. The romånce blends a dough where intellectual categories from the outside are challenged, which disturbs no one associated with prison literature; and there are no regrets that, in the poetic object arising from this kneading, the idea of a dialogue with official worlds is cruelly absent.

5. Formalism

Unlike the Shaggå, there exists no canonical model for the romånce. It can however be noted that the formalist dimension has been present from the beginning, from the first romånce, from the publication of *Minor Angels*, and that a preoccupation with metrical or musical order has always played a part in the constraints that authors are obliged to respect.

This formalism implements all sorts of formulae, none of which is considered better than any other.

While she reveals the number of words composing *Minor Angels* (sixty-six thousand six hundred sixty-six), Maria Clementi takes care to clarify that "so as not to harm the quality of the story," she desired to render this artifice invisible, "absolutely insignificant and imperceptible." In accord with this conception of writing, the authors of romånces will always give a discreet character to their formalist prowesses.

Despite that, one can easily find multiple examples. *White Night in Balkhyria* by Aidan Sherrad is comprised of forty-nine chapters, a magical number, a tantric number, very beautiful, around which dozens of sequential works will be constructed. Each capital letter at the beginning of the six

hundred sixty-six paragraphs in *Igor Euwe Calls Igor Euwe* by
Jean Vlassenko, when put together, creates a lyrical, astound-
ing, and harrowing subtext, through which the principal narrator's tortured companion expresses himself. *View Over the
Ossuary*, attributed to Jean Khorassan, is composed of two
rigorously-symmetrical parts, divided into texts that respond
to each other and include the same number of words, 1111,
777, 333 . . . *The Art of the Monologue in the Trenches* by Ralf
Thielmann has as its structure three hundred forty-three
sequences per page. Three hundred forty-three is, let us
recall, the cube of seven. Etc.

6. Orality

The fictional world of the romånce takes into account the
conditions in which the work will be circulated: recitation,
clandestine copy, whispering through doors. It takes them
into account and it reflects them.

The overnarrator imagines a distribution outside of the
walls, his romånce develops the notion of the text's exile.
The narrators know that a manipulation of the text will
occur elsewhere than in the high-security sector, and that
hands and minds will take possession of it, some of which
will certainly be devoid of any benevolence. This is why
the literary discourse of post-exoticism so easily follows
the sinuosities and ruptures of a police interrogation. Some
precautions are taken, in particular the encryption of names
and actions, along with a consistent narrative dodging that

does not reveal what the fictional logic would demand, speaks in a fallacious fashion, talks at length, solely to gain time—it *talks about something else.*

7. *Presence of the Reader*

Finally, the romånce introduces in itself, as an important element of the fiction, a representation of its reader. The true reader of the post-exotic romånce is one of the characters of post-exoticism.

No author forgets that readers exterior to post-exoticism, exterior to the high-security sector, sympathizers of every species, can venture into the post-exotic sphere. It is a perilous journey for them, with no chance of rescue, in the middle of obsessions and shames that none of their certainties at departure will help them to surmount. We see to it that they are welcomed into the closed world of the text and that they learn how to visit it without losing their sense of self.

But the readers addressed non-abstractly, those auditors animated by the fiction and before whom we murmur, and, even more so, the real male and female auditors to whom we dictate through the walls, do not need any road signs to travel unencumbered in our romånces. Those ones learn in the world of the high-security sector, and they share with us the labyrinths, the dysfunctions, and the absurd valors, and the fears, and the dreams, and the literatures.

IAKOUB KHADJBAKIRO

evoked the breath of a sick dog. The light had dimmed. From the other side of the grille, the yellow of the tape recorder's lamps had grown in substance. Subtitling a book "românce" was already in itself a violent parting from your universe, said Tarchalski. The Blotno somberly agreed. His blue eyes had lost all outspokenness. Without looking away from his notebook, he scratched all over the paper with flyfoot graffiti. His pages were covered in abundant material that should have satisfied him, but he looked disappointed by the turn the conversation had taken. I say that while thinking about the sweat running down his cheeks, which made him look like a panicking businessman on the losing end of an important deal. The conversation with the post-exotic authors wasn't building, didn't resemble an exchange at all, that's what was worrying the Blotno. It was going to be difficult to translate these demonstrations of bad humor, to adapt them to public taste; what was said here would not be appreciated on the outside. Not helping matters was the fact that Tarchalski's personality was escaping him more and more. His too-polite brutality had indisposed him from the start, and, now, it distressed him. To see the fawning demand for collusion the Blotno gave in glances at the sound taker is to understand how important the police and the notion of police were for the official critic's physical and mental tranquility. Tarchalski was perspiring in large drops as well, but for different reasons. Adrenaline was pulsing through his veins. It exasperated in him elementary needs for indignation and contempt that he had repressed for months, for want of finding an outlet, as for months he had had no interlocutor. He rose from the stool and approached the grille as if he were going to wrest it away while roaring.

Immediately, behind the door adjoining the room's airlock, resounded the voice of the guard in charge of discipline, an insolent voice, very hard. I no longer remember the name of that man, Batyrzian, or Kotter, or Otchaptenko, or Müller. Let's say it was Müller. Dimitri or John. A Müller worked in the high-security sector at the time. In an essay titled *So No One Gets Out*, Elia Fincke made a complete list of prison guards who took action against us from 1975 to 1999, and Müller is on there. With the hateful insolence of a beastmaster, Müller bellowed: Tarchalski! Return to your seat at once! And don't make any trouble or I'll send in the crew! The prisoner's pupils narrowed, they bored into the tape recorder's yellow light, the prisoner blanched, his hands blanched and froze a centimeter from the metal bars. And when I say "your universe" . . . he exhaled. Then he restrained himself, completely. He pretended to restrain himself, perhaps because he desired to contemplate for several more minutes, as if in a vivarium, this representative of an obscene species, this *Blotno non erectus* palpitating on the other side of the grille, or perhaps because he desired to distort the judgments that possible administration analysts might record in his file, and let them believe that sometimes he obeyed certain verbal menaces, that he was sensitive to reprimand. He sat back down on the stool, he scowled and stooped, and, for a moment, didn't say a word. The rain had invaded the soundscape. It streaked it, it imposed its falling scales on it, its muddy melodies, it took control of it, it choked it. Tarchalski remained passive, glued to his seat. He examined the creature breathing at least a meter away from him, a coward, submissive to his masters far or near. After a minute, the journalist made an imprecise gesture, as if he were erasing an imaginary chalkboard, and his irises once again oriented on Tarchalski. I immediately think that their base tint looked more Prussian than blue. I refused to meet those eyes, I was content to scrutinize the surrounding skin, the corners of his mouth, his temples, his eyebrows, his cheeks. Let's change the subject, the journalist proposed, and he mopped his brow, his nose, the bottom of his jaw. To everyone the air seemed foul, in the room reigned the odor of flatulence, of dirtied shirt. When I say "your universe," I know what I'm saying, whispered Tarchalski. Yesterday, to my colleague, intervened the Blotno with a small scrap of authority, Ellen Dawkes already made a statement on that subject. She has already confided in us her opinion on what separates us, in literature and in politics. On the existential incompatibility between you and . . . I doubt what she could have told you, Tarchalski rumbled, but, whether or not it pleases you, I have to repeat it. We repeat it nonstop. That is part of post-exoticism. He left his seat once more to press himself against the grille. The time for naturalistic observations was over. Anticipating what would follow, the policeman reached forward to reduce the device's sensitivity. Half a second passed. Outside, a flash of lightning streaked across the leaden shadow that had replaced the sky. Now, Yasar Tarchalski shook the grille with a theatrically devastating rage, which was dissipated uselessly into the iron, the concrete, the noise of the rain, and the thunder. We are elsewhere, we don't want to talk to you, you hear me, Blotno? . . . he yelled. Elsewhere! . . . None of us is speaking with you! . . . He had adopted the attitudes attributed to wild beasts in zoological gardens during times of despair or wrath, and, as the clubs beat down, his

5. Let's Talk about Something Else

We did not falter when we were hurt, we did not pretend to falter, we have pretended to be terrorized, we have not yelled our disarray on every pitch, our despair; instead of complaining we have composed long lists of birds, of decimated populations, of monkeys, of fishes, we have almost not mentioned the beatings we suffer, we have evoked other, more atrocious beatings that others have suffered, and, as a means of escape, we described blue countrysides, we have beaten wings above turquoise prairies, gliding over azure-colored barley, we have invented names for plants and small grasses, we have been moved deeply by the idea of these tiny plants, we have longed to sing of their veins and thus we have sung of them, we have almost never told the stories the enemy has been waiting for from us, most often we tell them far away, adopting a formalist point of view, literary in excess, barely corresponding to our taste, we have skirted central anecdotes so as not to inform the enemy of what really moves and pleases us, we have avoided handling the subjects we keep in our heads, from our actual memory we have only extracted anodyne information, we have not given the enemy the state of our political orientation, at no moment have we reproduced before the enemy any detail of the debates and instructions over which subcommissioners tenaciously excited themselves in the secret sections of their subcommissariats, we have permanently spooled false childhood memories, unusable biographies, nesting stories that abash and frustrate the enemy, that reveal nothing, that lead their specialized dogs astray, we have skimmed images of childhood at inopportune moments, we have inserted accounts of dreams where our spokespeople wanted confessions, we have not acted in accordance with the enemy's schedule, often we have declared that we were making efforts to clarify, with a very gesticulatory good will we have elaborated on love affairs vaguely police-related, giving the impression that we had finally accepted collaboration with the base culture of our torturers, but, in substance, we have used the wire-tapping capacity of our torturers and discouraged their intelligence, we have drowned it under fastidious scenes of black war, of espionage, placing our spies or our soldiers in inconceivable situations, we have constructed nocturnal countrysides that sometimes remain bathed in darkness from the first sentence to the last, we have accumulated nocturnal scenes that we have not illuminated, we have overdone the not-light despite the police demands and threats, we have not integrated into our behavior the idea that we must obey or answer, constantly we have avoided dialogue with those who received our proclamations or written declarations, when we are demanded a non-allegorical description of our crimes we have painted criminals at rest or retreating or in exile, characters who are only interested in clouds, and we have tried to reconstruct the fluctuating or fixed beauty of clouds, never have we accepted to write, to yell, or to say what was expected of us, preferring to invent, in the critical hours, large birds that disappear pair after pair into the backlighting, and loving madly these birds, pretending to have known them, to have known them well, to have studied their chatter and their cries, to have suffered with them, and when I say suffer I am not speaking lightly, and, every time one or another of us perished, our tale marked a pause, we have stopped, we have interested ourselves in things smaller still than our adventure, less significant still, more absurd than our suffering, and we have roared in high voices the remains of texts that prevented us from believing our pain had any importance, we have spit on them with what carried on our high voices in plain malice, we have filled the countryside with brusque enthusiasms on the microscopic level, of the most sordid kinds, we have devised meticulous reports on the pitiable and on mere nothings, we have raised ourselves up in favor of less than nothing, we made our narration walk on transversal roads, we modified the inhuman shrieking in our throats and we turned it into a variation the enemy refused to read and did not even have the desire to decode, so removed was it from the atrocious groaning they were finally ready to understand. We have always talked about something else, always.

ELLEN DAWKES

sentences became disorganized. When I say "the enemy" . . . "you" . . . I know what . . . The Blotno mopped his cheeks with a handkerchief. He had observed Tarchalski's beating without commentary. There was a silence. And if we finally addressed the animal themes, fraternization with the beasts, the Blotno continued. If we take interest in that, eh? . . . The question was for Irina Kobayashi, whom the guards had dragged to the stool. Large hailstones lashed against the reinforced glass window, as if someone were throwing gravel, in great fistfuls, with pointless persistence. What day was it again? Maybe April sixteenth, since it wasn't yet the seventeenth, the anniversary of Wolfgang Gardel's suicide, by fire, in cell 234. Irina Kobayashi sneezed, and then took from her pants pocket a square of cloth into which she blew her nose. There are numerous post-exotic authors who place an animal presence at the heart of their narrations, said the journalist. Yesterday, Yasar Tarchalski was about to discuss his theory on the subject, but the interview got off course . . . We were interrupted . . . He didn't . . . He had just gotten to the theme of birds, of his experiences in the forest, in the equatorial world . . . It's obsessional, for him, for you, by all evidence . . . The birds, but not only . . . Other, larger animals . . . or smaller . . . According to the stories . . . Irina Kobayashi raised onto him eyes yellowed and cloudy with fever. She was ill. Insects, spiders, crabs, the Blotno listed. Frequently, your narrators rant in front of these kinds of bugs . . . And there are also these bizarre characters, whose non-humanity is manifest, in whom you entrust a central role . . . They take the floor and direct the fiction . . . Examples . . . The Blotno flipped through his notebook, in search of indisputable titles, but his notes were of no help. He was lost, the paper rustled, he was confused. There is no lack of examples, he said. Often . . . The precise species and order of animal to which the heroes belong is unknown, he added. Irina Kobayashi let the journalist's muttering run its course. Outside, the rain blossomed into rhythms and sub-rhythms, seven-stroke bombardments, compound splashes. She listened to this music as she judged that phantom of official power, whose intelligence stumbled over the most luminous elements of post-exoticism. And you? she asked. What, me? the Blotno started. Outside, said Irina, your world is nothing. Your world is a hell for humans as well as animals . . . One infernal circus among others, an example of illusion and nothingness. Hardly touched by the fever, Irina's voice suddenly swelled, a superb singer's voice, whose inflections made us tremble every time they roamed the fifth floor of the high-security unit from cell 1459. And on top of that, she continued, you have, in the intention of collaborating with those responsible for this evil, those who entitled you to exist as mercenaries in the first place, you have grafted from the romanesque antidepressant, from perfumed speech, a whole arsenal of . . . She stood up, as always when a heroine or madwoman of post-exoticism begins to apostrophize the nothingness. The reel of the tape recorder shot up at the same time, the tape had ended or was broken, the policeman thrust toward the mechanism his chest, his slugger hands, his hard-hitting face. And you, Blotno how? . . . Blotno what? . . . said Irina Kobayashi. To what order do you belong? . . . Whose barker are you? . . . Who feeds you? . . . Who are you? . . . The conversation continued like such. According to the place we got to, there were, throughout the galleries we took to reach the parlor, tears or laughter of the rain and wind. I took pleasure in this walk, like through the passageways of a ship in a storm, lamenting the

6. Novelles or Interjoists

With the romånce and the Shaggå, novelles offer post-exoticism a third type of original support, as powerful as those that precede it and as frequently used. Once again, the author must adapt his inspiration to a controlled space, but without letting the constraint unbalance the quality of his discourse. Immense developments and microscopic fables coexist under the heading of novelle; the airiest poetry can be found, such as Anita Negrini's, alongside brutalistic realism, like Petra Kim's.

Behind the system that governs the novelle's function, one will find several common traits shared with other genres of post-exoticism: 1) a similar record of difference with the outside; 2) a similar will to widen this fracture, to accentuate the gap with the real world, perceived as being the source of all sorrow; 3) a similar worry over proclaiming its dissidence in comparison to the fashions flourishing outside the penal ghetto.

Collections of novelles include texts in pairs. Each pair makes up an ensemble that Khrili Gompo, in the preface to his founding work *Façade Restoration*, has proposed be baptized *interjoist*.

The term interjoist is a fortunate one. It suggests magical practices, a conjuration, and, at the same time, a musical intimacy, made of interlaced fantasizing, reciprocity, and division; it brings into evidence the circular nature of this structure, its simple and solid curvature.

Let us look a little closer.

A primary text, the *novelle*, creates a literary domain. The subject often has rapport with the fantastical, but not always. A situation is defined, characters act, the anecdote disagrees on a precise cultural web, with its implicit past and what it leaves unsaid. A second text, called the *annex* or the *response*, takes possession of a moment chosen in the body of the preceding narration and makes it prosper, though not in seeking to clarify or complete the first tale: it is a second piece of prose with an independent character and its own literary objectives, its own style, its own reserve of archives and images. Nevertheless, the set falls into a binary narrative system. The sole presence of the response is enough for the literary domain to gain in coherence. A network of harmonics takes consistency, the images circulate better, the story resonates better, deeper; what remains unsaid cannot be confused with omissions, it has at present a poetic status. The existence of two associated texts places on the set a thick supplementary veil of meaning.

From the subconscious of the author to the subconscious of the reader, something is equally framed, which is not the least of the interjoist's achievements. The twisted, curved, autonomous universe underpinning and justifying the two interjoisted tales stretches seamlessly beyond the text, and, in the world of the sympathizing, receptive reader, it replaces reality. References to the outside world wither away, they lose a good portion of their pertinence. In order to appreciate the interjoist, to roam it and inhabit it, it is no longer useful to dwell on exterior ideological and aesthetic categories.

Reading a collection of interjoists reinforces the post-exotic certainty of being "between self," far from loquacious mastiffs, propagandists, and millionaire entertainers. The literary domain of the interjoist opens onto the infinite: it becomes a travel destination, a haven for the narrator, a land of exile, tranquil exile, for the reader, out of the enemy's reach, forever out of the enemy's reach.

ERDOGAN MAYAYO

absence of swaying and quietly stumbling so as to recreate it. The conversation continued like such, advancing the cause of progressive literature. Irina Kobayashi passed away that same year, from a hemorrhage she suffered when someone slashed her knuckles to the bone. As always when one of our own was murdered, we formed a community bearing her name. Her voice resonated with ours, inside ours. Her memory continued to exist, to mix in thoughts we could claim as our own, and it continued to create images where we moved with happiness, dreams that denied reality and subverted it. Irina Kobayashi's two final works are admirable: *Low Waters, Waters Very Low*, a sweeping, symphonic, deeply moving romånce about extermination, and *Dangerous Verbiage*, a collection of lyrical interjoists, also of breathtaking splendor. Several of us disappeared in those days: Jean Khorassan, Verena

Nordstrand, Rita Hoo, William Lethbridge, Vassilissa Lukaszczyk.
Like all those who had preceded them on the list of the dead, we
paid them homage. In the high-security sector, the survivors have
always considered that they could serve as vocal and physical support to the intelligence of those who no longer answered calls.
For example, we resuscitated the poetic vein of Verena Nordstrand, spitting on the world of the enemy her imprecations and
inimitable slogans; or we imitated Vassilissa Lukaszczyk's style to
breathe fire into recitacts spoken before our cells' sanitary tiling; or
else, we dramatized Jean Khorassan and Rita Hoo in interjoists
and romånces. All of us endeavored to prolong their terrestrial
presence. Personalities changed, signatures blended together like
blood bonds: we sometimes would print the names of the deceased beneath the texts we composed; or, conversely, we laid
claim loud and clear to crimes, or books, authored by our disappeared brothers and sisters. We passed the time soliloquizing in
this fashion, between life and death, always knowing how to distinguish in the secrets of even the shortest sentences what was
born of the heteronymy and what took part in the orthonymy,
but hardly concerning ourselves with making a remark on the
subject. It was however desirable and useful to explore the question, I mean useful for post-exoticism, for our literature. Around
that spring, Irina Kobayashi's last, Lutz Bassmann tackled this the-
oretical task. He invented the concepts of mute voice, under-
narrator, fictive speech, counter-voice, dead voice, sub-realism,
polychrony, narrative apnea, etc. All these notions immediately
facilitated analysis of our texts and helped us to appreciate them,

and to improve their melodic capacity, and to. And to. And to love them even more. They clung to the true nature of our quixotic poetry and they allowed us to evaluate successes and failures, an exercise that was often a struggle for the tools we sometimes borrowed from the official critics' junk box. By the end of the millennium, several debates had taken place, enriching Bassmann's proposed terminology. Their unfolding has been depicted in a handful of românces, such as *Summation Number Zero, A Hen at Bloudy-Mongo's*, or *Autopsy of a Korean Woman*, so let us not mention here once again how our books circulated, despite the bannings and material obstacles, and despite the illnesses that life in prison instilled in us, despite this weight of time that clouded our perceptions and accelerated our physical and psychic decrepitude. Lutz Bassmann had dissected already-existing techniques. His definitions applied to post-exotic literature since its inception, they illuminated every fantastical work that had come before, every narrator's often-ambiguous ruminations and dealings. They were put into practice, they were integrated like a jigsaw into the poetic creation process by authors from the third and fourth generations, such as Raïa Ossorguina, Oleg Damtew, Mario Hinz, Elli Kronauer, Sonia Velazquez, Hans-Jürgen Pizarro, Manuela Draeger, and many others. Whenever some critical remark would strip down the most intimate defenses from the collective edifice we had constructed—or rather, that each one of us in his or her harrowing solitude had contributed to constructing—an undeniable sensation of fullness irrigated the post-exotic productions. It does not matter whose signature is giving the piece material consistence, be it an

7. Specific Terms

We all know that it is hazardous to analyze the post-exotic production with terms conceived by official literary critics, made for performing autopsies on the textual cadavers that riddle their morgues. The exercise is possible, though at the price of mental contortions that turn post-exoticism into a meeting place for the schizophrenic and haughty elite, perversely infatuated with illegible music.

The traditional critic's analytic sifting has this effect: it deceives, but, above all, it makes hideous and it kills. Unadapted instruments lacerate and overwrite the text, they do not succeed in dismantling the machinery, they rely on fields of logic that we have only touched upon, for example the aesthetic status of the narrator, and they neglect what we consider essential, like the speaking voice's degree of degradation, or its romantic relationship with the memory of Wernieri, Maria Schrag, or Maria Clementi, etc., or the angle of attack by which our heroes expose their hatred for the enemy.

Furthermore, recourse to tools belonging, ultimately, to a different kind of science swaddles our texts in a reasoning unable to abstract them from the contemporary artistic movement and, to the contrary, drives them away in an abusive, disloyal fashion, one which is perfectly absurd. For lack of finding a convincing place for post-exoticism, it is relegated to the avant-gardes, to whom, it must be said, it shares the same relation with as it does with the rest of the non-incarcerated world. Post-exoticism is a literature coming from elsewhere and going elsewhere, an *alien literature* that welcomes various leanings and tendencies, many of which reject sterile avant-gardism. That is what we must make our critics aware of.

We need a specific critical vocabulary.

I propose we look into the definition of the following terms, though this list should not be considered exhaustive:

Terms Concerning the Qualification of Voices:
overnarrator
under-narrator
anonymous heteronym
mute voice
counter-voice
dead voice

Terms Tied to the Nature of the Language:
fictive speech
decorative phrasing
blackletter
crypt language

Terms Explaining the Treatment of the Subject or Sentence:
narrative scansion
narrative watermark
narrative fluttering

anecdotal web

chronological apnea

polychrony

double arch

simple delinquency

cyclical collusion

reticular progression

micro-theatricality

paradoxical colorization

musical mass

pseudo-mass

Terms Reflecting Particularities of the Fiction:

homage

spiral landscape

imprecatory focus

residual anecdote

temporal mask

oneiric mask

We could, in the framework of this exploration, acquire a better understanding of ourselves. This will not completely appease us, for knowing does not help with living, nor with speaking, but it will at least encourage us to meet our ends less ineptly.

LUTZ BASSMANN

announced or anonymous author, a figurehead, a spokesperson, a heteronym, a collective, a deadman, or a deadwoman; the post-exotic voice sang in a style totally devoid of incoherence or dependence, which is to say that fewer than before were seeking to confront the official poetic universe or non-incarcerated reality as a way of affirming their particularity. Erdogan Mayayo, in a didactic talk he whispered just before he was silenced by a gravity knife under the sink in cell 891, explained how the conscience of *being between self* influenced post-exoticism's structural choices. The *between self* conducted words and images capable of finding their light, their nuances, their heat, their history, and their function where we had no exit. The *between self* conscience wiped the slate clean of architectural norms that, outside, the madness of the Nioukis and Blotnos would never edit, out of either a fear of falling sales or natural sheepishness. Lutz Bassmann spoke of a *limpid hermeticism* that skimmed our fantastical symphonies. On questions of vocabulary we disputed for a long time, for example over this notion of hermeticism that some of us thought pejorative, or too slavishly modeled on the enemy's aesthetic categories; but, if I had to characterize the spirit of this period, I would say that we were firmly united above all, partners in everything, and unfazed, taken with a stupefying serenity only understood by conquerors. It is true that, in the literary domain, we had undertaken the objectives of the first generation. We were upstarts in a golden age and, at the heart of our texts, the enemy was no more than a fragile shadow over whom we held the power of life and death. Outside was nothing but a literary invention, a virtual world that we fashioned or destroyed as we pleased. This feeling of infinite intellectual freedom perhaps came as well from the fact that the outside world was no longer interested in the prisoners of the high-security sector, or their literature. Outside, the secular world had sunk into atrocious conflicts, removed more and more from the "egalitarianism or barbarism" binary that had inspired, that had illuminated our crimes during the seventies and eighties. Barbarism having triumphed on every level, the idea of fighting to get rid of it had become so foreign to official ideologues, so abstruse, that the convictions we still held onto in the prison universe no longer meant anything to them. No one led attacks against our basic program anymore and no one crossed swords with our highest program to eradicate the causes of suffering anymore, either. The media had relegated egalitarianism to the rank of causes not only lost, but obsolete and forgotten. The era cared so little about denouncing our misdeeds, or attacking our ideological archaisms, that our apprehended sympathizers found themselves subjected to psychiatric treatments rather than imprisonment alongside us in available cells in the high-security sector, on floors empty from suicides and those put to death. We came to realize that the concentration camp system where we were locked up was egalitarian utopia's ultimate impregnable fear, the only terrestrial space whose inhabitants were still fighting for a variant of paradise. In the imaginary world of our golden age, beggars in solitary confinement were more and more often made protagonists in our romånces, a role that we used to reserve for warriors and armed prophets, for all those fantastic and subversive voyagers we

8. A Murmuract:
"Breughel Calls Clementi"

When all we were had been removed, even the masks, we listened to Clementi's songs. We had ended up in garbage dumps or in prison, we were buried in obliviating ashes, and we listed the dead: Maria Schrag, Siegfried Schulz, Inge Albrecht, the Katalina Raspe commune, the Verena Goergens commando unit, Infernus Iohannes, Breughel, the Ingrid Schmitz commune, and many others. The poets of subversion were nothing more than shadows. Outside, the masters sent their dogs to search through the ruins we inhabited, and they ordered their clowns to obnoxiously dirty the speeches we gave in the heart of the flames. These were the moments of distress when we most felt the need to hear an echo of what had been, in another time, our existences. We assembled ourselves with difficulty, groping about, we crossed again together the darkness's first dark ordeals, at our memory's peril we roamed dusty streets, ruins, long swamps of soot and, finally, we found the path to the room, and we pushed open the door. A handful of waggish survivors had filled their empty eye sockets, below their eyelids or above, with grayish pebbles, smoothed stones, with the idea of dramatizing from this a hopeless simulacrum of courage. With deep affection we took each other by the hand in the darkness, then formed a pile in the depths of the cave, in affectionate harmony. From time to time, in order to notify others of their position, those with stones took them from their quarters and knocked them together, saying: Siegfried Schulz calls Clementi, please respond, or: Katalina Raspe calls Clementi, please respond. Sometimes the door to the room would open abruptly, the hinges creaked, the panel banged against the wall. We stopped speaking. A flashlight was shone here and there in the thick emptiness, searching for stowaways or forbidden writings. As nothing differentiated us from the debris, the investigators did not detect our presence, and the door was closed once again. After an hour or two of vigilance, one of us would start again, saying: Breughel calls Clementi, please respond. Then, in the heart of the darkness, the music was born, very intense, overcoming organic boundaries and penetrating each person sometimes from the room's interior, sometimes from the refuge of our skulls. We murmured a few terrible phrases, formerly made by autumn monks and dissidents, we whispered chants of dread for the Ingrid Schmitz commune, then we curled up in increased solidarity. Clementi's music offered its architecture to our forms, Clementi's music recomposed what had been destroyed and sullied in us, our broken and dirtied childhoods, the dreams that the masters' animals or official clowns had distorted or soiled. Throughout the rhythms, we began again to exist in our envelopings even more hermetically. We were holding onto each other by the meat of our fingers, by the flesh of our palms, and by the memory, suddenly inaccessible and immobile, dancing invulnerably, in scarves of fire, marbled black in the black transparencies of the fire, from image to image wandering and from one dream to the other, exiled, disguised as birds of stone and eagles of blood, always clothed in rags, sleeping breathlessly, mendicant, beyond any length of time, of adventures and combat, then once again subjected to temporal measurements, trembling with beauty, so touched we were. A phenomenon was produced that we named *intersailing* or *vault swelling* and the music allowed access to the same dreamlike universes that reciting poems did. We marveled at being able to take up the journey that other men and women had completed, out of friendship for us, in solitude and violence, whose vestiges we humbly wished to honor. Clementi's music resuscitated these vestiges and gave us the power to recite them. Sometimes I rose in the shadows of the room, bumping against those who had survived but didn't move, listening to what continued to rumble and endlessly persist, the pendulum of an ocean in the obstinacy of our heads, the respiration of a narrator in the silence of our bony oscillations. I rose, I knocked together pebbles chafed by tears, I went to open the door. It was dark. I wanted to pursue the struggle, now that the music had breathed enough energy into me to struggle and to pursue. I made sure no one was walking in the street, I sat down in front of the door, I stayed there for a long time, sitting or crouching. I started

> again my attack on the pebbles and I let my voice flow, say-
> ing: Breughel calls Clementi, please respond, or: Breughel
> here, it's very dark, please respond.
>
> ELLI KRONAUER

tenderly accompanied, put into texts, and adored. Rooms with no
exit became frequent, and in certain years, like 2003 and 2004, they
gave way to no other theme. The hermetic enclosure could vary,
physical confinement here, psychic imprisonment there, forbidding
liberation through dreams, like in Roman Nachtigall's fearsome
Saving Black Marfa, or in *Liars' Bridge* by Monika Domrowski, but,
in general, the characters and narrators no longer harbored any
nostalgia behind the scenes. We had stripped the landscape of its
exterior. The prison was defined by Manuela Draeger as a *lesser
hell*. When one of us was liberated prematurely, which is to say
before the end of his or her agony, he immediately put himself to
death or arranged to be killed: he or she. The notice of death took
some time to reach us, for, in compliance with an old police mea-
sure from the eighties, the newspapers the administration allowed
us to read had to have first rotted in a cellar for eight months
before joining the library shelves. But a new photograph ended up
pinned or scotched to our walls, somewhere on the partitions of
this parallel universe . . . somewhere in this closed place where our
utopia, well beyond its sinking, flourished, grew radiantly, shone,
recuperated, suffered from rare illnesses, neither infantile nor
senile and until then undescribed, wallowed in nightmares,

degenerated, regenerated, floated between two dreams. We examined the portraits of our dead friends and spoke to them, no longer writing our texts on paper, introducing more and more silence and words unsaid into the romanesque clay with which we modeled the fates of beings who had been fraternal variants of ourselves. More spontaneously than during the preceding decades, our narrators began to form with us and with his or her own characters an insoluble sense of self. This evolution of post-exoticism toward a less baroque, narrower, and more compact system, with more intimist stories, can be traced back to the first ten years of the new millennium. Disregarding the case of blackletter poems, our language remained confined to a less sophisticated register than before, though perhaps more humble. In romånces and murmuracts from the two thousands, readers and auditors beyond these walls could follow along without perplexity, if by chance they were given the opportunity to follow along. The texts dating from this period are marvels of limpid hermeticism. They are whisperable by the non-living and the living alike, by anyone still inclined to crumbs of voice and love. Very few bridges are established anymore between post-exoticism and official literature, that which does not prevent the murmur of heteronyms from being audible to any ear, perceptible to every intelligence. Of course, the ambition to be read or heard by others than ourselves no longer entertained us. The idea of artistic competition, or even parallel development, was no longer suitable to explain the existing relationship between us and those outside our camp. There was no longer any relationship. We lived on too-different planets, too distant from each other for any sort of semblance of contact. And already, we . . . Because we had traveled a very long road of isolation, of rumination, it was harder and harder for us to persuade ourselves that our group and the people on the outside belonged to the same community. On the genetic level, it also seemed to us that a discrepancy had come about. We felt alien to the human populations we mixed with on our journeys, in our books, when we traveled in dreams, when we began visiting the outside to witness the triumph of the capitalist order and its wars. When the echoes of nationalist massacres or the figures of poverty or other ignominies reached us, and they arrived constantly, we had to translate them into our own images and xenoliterary metaphors in order to accept and comprehend them. New terms were devised by the latest spokespeople to clarify this subtle change to our mood, our points of view, and our tastes. In her preface to *The Hunt for the Mocking Platonov*, Rebecca Wolff comments on the new poetic strategies of post-exoticism while drawing on concepts from a manual on animal psychology she borrowed from the prison library. The following year, in the (truth be told, very, very depressed) preface to his final work, *The Pharaohs before the Door*, Mario Hinz tries to move our literary sensibilities to the realm of the non-human. He undertakes a rereading of post-exoticism in light of a xenopsychiatric theory. The terms appearing in these studies are not, in my opinion, always adequate, and they pose more problems than they resolve, but the intuition is right. A new literary stage has debuted. Calling on imaginary masses and animals as witnesses, careful not to intellectually shock the spiders nesting in their cells, post-exotic authors continue to describe parallel elsewheres and a beyond, as they have done since the beginning of their literature, but the nature of this beyond has changed. Something has enriched or impoverished the detained overnarrators' mental universe. Their supernatural can no longer be correctly elucidated or depicted with properly human expressive techniques, what I mean by that . . . What I mean is *Homo sapiens*, but also "human" in the sense of a confidant and . . . and referential entity . . . Though it is affirmed text after text, the coincidence of our preoccupations with humanity's hopes and future had lost any sign of credibility. That fact reveals itself more and more often in our fictions, for example in Manuela Draeger's romånces, where inexplicable anomalies in her characters' behaviors, alongside discretionary errors and mental incongruities, constantly accrue, making the certainty of the author's terrestrial roots uncertain. Rebecca Wolff and Mario Hinz's critical work was a dead-end. Nonetheless, it had the virtue of lucidly indicating what would be the final period of post-exoticism. Between post-exotic voices and the very concrete planet where they could have rung out, but where they were met with neither applause nor welcome by anyone or anything, the ties became progressively reduced into a sham of solidarity, into a soft, inconsistent moral obligation. Facing the essentially bipedal and essentially murderous population completely enchanted by capitalist bestiality, we too felt like bipeds and murderers, but also foreigners, in service to a parallel civilization, bearing another intelligence and another blood . . . The distance grew . . . We felt closer and closer to . . . In the end, it is useless to speculate on this metamorphosis that, maybe, the first generation had judged frightening, and that we only found curious. The romånces of Manuela Draeger, the most corrosive of which being *Hospice Exchange*, are, above all, fictions of an extraordinary originality, and it would be a grave injustice to speak of it as if I were a teratologist unmoved by his object of study. After Manuela Draeger was immolated, her romånces were murmured and sputtered with love by the handful of detainees who still survived in the high-security sector . . . They were claimed without the slightest hint of any grudge . . . I can clearly recall Lutz Bassmann's voice reciting *Departure to Detachment*, Maria Sauerbaum's exhaling line-after-line the *Shaggås of Vertiginous Nostalgia* . . . Someone else's . . . Someone was also reading wearily their own masterwork . . . *A Lama on the East Coast* . . . attributing it to Manuela Draeger . . . I would like at present, since I still have the floor, to express myself on the mystical and monastic aspects of post-exotic solitude and on the bonds we have maintained with magic and theories of shamanic voyage that permit a visit to the lands before death: before or after birth or death. Accompanied by a variety of sacrileges, since each of us adapted them to the profane demands of his or her own narration, the intoxicating ramblings of tantrism were the spiritual air that post-exotic characters inhaled and exhaled, while egalitarianism was the raspy political breath in their lungs. I do not know when, exactly, this double respiration found its rhythm. Outside the walls, in our adolescence, in embryonic form . . . or later, when we had already begun down the path of political crime, and when, after having beaten the enemy, we went back there in dreams . . . when, covered in blood, in dreams we sought refuge and rest in sumptuous totalitarian

9. Two Words on Our Bardo and Its Thödol

I would now like to say a few words on the mystical and monastic aspects of post-exotic solitude and on the bonds we have maintained with magic and theories of magical, shamanic voyage, that so often resonate at the center of our fanciful apparatus.

From its earliest proses, indeed, our literature has used notions such as cyclical fate, non-death death and non-life life, transmigration, and reincarnation, and it has given support to the action in the form of a reality made of multiple worlds, illusory and parallel. Post-exotic writers have described crossing dark space, the tetanization of time, walking through fire or in pain: the entire gamut of ordeals through which the chasms of time and space are vanquished. With great ease and since the beginning, characters in their books create pathways and portals from one soul to another, they wander from one dream to another, they slip from one universe to another. Post-exotic fiction rests on such crossings.

That does not mean that blows are brought to the intransigent and pure materialism required of egalitarianism. Indeed, if the authors put reality in doubt, their skepticism does not rely on a religious conception of the visible or invisible. They know that no divine power skulks behind the mysteries of the world. They give no faith to the idea that some enchanting sphere, miraculously exempt from evil and stupidity, exists somewhere to receive the privileged. They often regret having to deny, but they are nihilists.

This morose heathenism is transmitted to every speaker and tragedian animated in our stories. An identical absolute nihilism can be found in them, whatever their level of responsibility on the fiction's scale, if one examines the thoughts of overnarrators, anonymous heteronyms, or the most obscure spokesmen.

There are still however numerous shamans and priors in post-exotic literature, along with magicians, necromancers, telepaths, and a full gallery of those privileged to overcome eternity and overstep the threshold of reality and death as they please. But even these are beings who do not profess the smallest amount of belief. They do not worship any given power, excepting the Great Brood, about which we shall mutter a few words later on. They consider themselves to be atheistic technicians, artisans of transmigration, and strangers to every religious community.

One cannot deny that certain characters invest their imprecations with the high patronage of the Great Brood, and invoke with fervor its most terrifying figures, its ladies and lords of the first order, as well as hierarchically dilapidated angels, like the *windy ones*, the *Delphic clowns*, or the *third-wave chrysalides*. A pantheon is therefore active in proximity to these speakers, likely influencing their fate and, in any case, hearing their prayers. However, if one looks closer, one perceives that the Great Brood is only ever treated as a local occult bureaucracy. When one is aggrieved to outline, based on information distilled from its zealots, a coherent cosmogony, one quickly arrives at the conclusion that the Great Brood is nothing. Lady Left Death only appears throughout two or three accepted curses, given by non-believers, and the rest of the Great Brood occupies solely non-universal territories, hermetic globes where the nightmares of insane mediums boil.

In reality, under the same heading as permanent revolution, universal gravitation, or xenophilia, atheism is one of our entry-level intellectual gifts, composed of foundational evidence not worth mentioning, and even less so dismantling at every opportunity.

However, in parallel, an acute religiosity haunts our fictions, a religiosity so strong and sincere that it transforms the daily behavior of our narrators and drives them to monastic attitudes: meditation, silence, the ritualization of existence's gestures, a morality of compassion and shared suffering, speeches for the dead, and magical accompaniment of the deceased through their voyage toward rebirth.

These behaviors have two origins.

The first comes from a lifetime of reclusion, in isolated cells, which makes wall-facing rumination and other monastic conduct completely natural.

The second is the noted influence of a book that circulated among us at one moment in our adventure, in the eighties, the *Bardo Thödol* or *Tibetan Book of the Dead*.

Julio Sternhagen, in charge of the library at the time, right before his hanging, had gotten it in from the outside, along with teaching material and several popularized works on Buddhism. The administration, perhaps because they were already planning Julio Sternhagen's suicide and desired to anesthetize their victim's distrust, or mislead future investigators, had approved this request. The book was quickly a huge success among us, for it coincided splendidly with our poetic virtues: 1) The description of hell was quite like what we had undertaken, in our own way, from our first writings; 2) The idea of a conscious journey through death, a walk sowed with pitfalls and discourse, which drove the cadaver, or what remained of it, toward failure, that is to say toward rebirth, suited us; 3) Our plots and characters had always blossomed in narrative systems where non-duality and non-opposition between opposites reigned; 4) Eternity was our daily lot, no one more than us had ever experienced its ravages; 5) Discourse with the dead was what we had put into practice since post-exoticism's beginning, since our bodies had been collectively padlocked; 6) The book itself, with its commentaries, functioned like ours, at the same time on a plane of writing and a plane of orality; and 7) It had circulated for centuries from hand to hand among the tattered and miserable, whom we had no difficulty taking as models, or making fraternize with our characters.

Julio Sternhagen hanged himself, some of us imitated him, the library closed, and book lending was interrupted for several years. The copy of the *Bardo Thödol* had made its way into Maria Schnittke's cell.

In a frail voice, cracked with weariness, Maria Schnittke dedicated months to its chanting before the hatch in her door, door 1157, until every one of us could repeat it by heart and transmit it in turn. This episode of active whispering of a non-post-exotic text never happened again, it is unique, it lastingly influenced the incarcerated universe and it forever marked the universes we invented, the cities, the countrysides, the oceans, and the deserts we made to escape the high-security sector and continue to exist somewhere, in some other hell, together.

In some other reality, fictive or not, falsely tantric or not, but together.

The *Bardo Thödol* is for us a referential text from which we have eroded every truly Buddhist dimension and that we have reconstructed according to our individual and collective sensibilities, in order to adapt it to our literature, for it to help our characters live their non-lives and cross their non-deaths. It is a magnificent text, whose every song embellishes our voices and whose every image and explanation satisfy and console us, and accompany us, assist us, reassure us, frighten us, keep us awake, launch us toward the unknown, encourage us to still move, rob us of our laughter, amuse us, fulfill us, and inspire us.

YASAR TARCHALSKI

sanctuaries, imaginary worlds endlessly fenced . . . flawlessly encircled . . . protected from exterior enmity by every species of barbed wire intelligence had ever conceived of . . . or later still, inside the incarcerated world . . . I don't know when . . . To say with clarity, I would have to search through remote existences . . . too far away now, too faded . . . Stir up the sludge of memory that is now mixed with oneiric shreds, with unreadable dregs . . . I can only recall those long weeks Maria Schnittke dedicated to the transmission of the *Bardo Thödol* . . . The humidity . . . Dampness seeped from the walls, the ceiling dripped, invaded by darker-than-dark mold. Everything was mottled with black mysteries. We perspired near our doors, one ear glued to the hatch, murmuring, so we could adapt the heavy prayers and reprimands that make up the *Book of the Dead*. We received it night and day, without interruption, with moments of pedagogical revision during which parts of the text were repeated by Maria Schnittke or the following links in the sonic chain that formed from Maria Schnittke's cell. We could not escape phases of drowsiness or sleep, during which the text's continuity continued, so that in our plunge back into consciousness, when we shook ourselves from our vapors, there was the impression that we had already witnessed the *Thödol*'s whole recitation, elsewhere, at another time, in a dream or somewhere else, whether we had been the monk reading the book at a dead person's bedside, or we had lain impassively, beneath the flood of words describing worlds, the exterior's successive hells, and the interior's labyrinths, and explaining by what method to escape them. If you want to see things objectively, the *Bardo Thödol* has

---

never been and will never be a sacred text to us, a manual full of religious content, delivering messages to the initiated and the devout. It is a text intimately tied to the voices of post-exoticism, a fiction whose tantric esotericism conceals no revelation. The *Bardo Thödol* is a post-exotic text, meant exclusively for the members of the high-security sector, and transmitted from prisoner to prisoner, in an atmosphere of love, secrecy, and fear. It is spoken by Maria Schnittke from cell 1157 . . . And now . . . Now, only Lutz Bassmann could still deliver it. He murmured it facing our photographs, while agony mounted inside him like a tide and while odors of rot grew on the outside of his pulmonary sacs and on the inside of his narrative emissions. The rain drummed ferociously on the window. It was April, the end of April or the beginning of May, or maybe November. The world was sticky. Beads of sweat flowed down Lutz Bassman's forehead. Besides the *Bardo Thödol*, there remained one more book to speak, a romånce he had to cite, which would respond perfectly to the first post-exotic text, *Minor Angels* by Maria Clementi, and which—a book that would close the edifice and make Maria Clementi's voice, alongside her closest comrades and friends, resonate in rebirth one last time. And after, darkness would fall forever over the first generation, over them and over us. It was necessary to construct a new fiction to rejoin the final tar and finally balance and close everything. *Return to the Tar* was thus born, most likely. The romånce took back the themes that Maria Clementi—once again Moyocoatzin and Mlatelpopec appeared, as well as Gardel and the heroes to whom we had never ceased to forever give homage, from the beginning of that long, that interminable march beneath the lead, in thick silence, through the nothingness of human history, outside the outside. Once again from the dark space emerged my madmen, my killers. My forever favorite killers and . . . Maria Schrag, Maria Soudayeva, Julio Sternhagen, Soudayev, Wernieri. Better than everything and everyone . . . They reemerged, relived, reinflamed, redied. Words escaped our lips, words which already no longer coincided with an abstract act of creation. When I say "our" lips, I am distorting reality in a way that carries no consequence, since no one was there to. No one was there to witness this distortion. Poetic artifices accumulated on the tiles, at the foot of the bed, like lumps of dust. As for the images and acoustic inventions, no one would be bothered to revive them with sympathy. It was getting harder and harder to distinguish meaning from them or their reason for existing. Maria Schrag's adventure, Wernieri's, hissed a millimeter above the ground, among dirty granules, in the currents of fetid humidity. *Return to the Tar* possessed the qualities of a powerful românce, and I believe that it could have been a manifestation of post-exoticism's inventive vitality, but it rang, so feebly, more or less without an author and without an audience, for nothing. The immense prison moaned like a rat-abandoned, crewless ship, one that would soon sink. In the corridors, the wind blew, and sometimes, prophesying the last sentence on which post-exotic breath would stop, it grew silent. It was difficult to establish a border between the sounds of water made by the deluge, Bassmann's death rattles made by Bassmann, and the simulacrums of memory made by the photographs of those who had been our overnarrators. Post-exoticism ended there. The cell smelled like the decomposed world, burning humus, terminal fever, it plagued the fears that the most humble animals, and I am sorry for it, never found the words to describe. There was no longer a single spokesperson to come after. So I am the one who

10. By the Same Author, in the Same Collection

1. MINOR ANGELS, *ROMÂNCE*, MARIA CLEMENTI, 1977

2. MOLDSCHER, *ROMÂNCE*, MARIA IGUACEL, 1977

3. SCENERY PRIOR TO HANGING, *ROMÂNCE*, JULIO STERNHAGEN, 1978

4. GOLSHEM ADVANTAGE, *ROMÂNCE*, JULIO STERNHAGEN, 1978

5. THE DREAMS THINK, *ROMÂNCE*, MARIA AROSTEGUI, 1978

6. A BALKHYRIAN OPERA, *ROMÂNCE*, MARIA IGUACEL, 1979

7. MIRRORS OF THE CADAVER, *SHAGGÂS*, INFERNUS IOHANNES, 1979

8. THE ANNULMENT OF THE NEW YEAR, *ROMÂNCE*, WERNIERI, 1979

9. MYRIAM'S SILENCE, *SHAGGÂS*, JEAN WOLGUELAM, 1979

10. SOLDIERS, *ROMÂNCE*, ANTON BREUGHEL, 1979

11. THE ABACAU'S MURMUR, *ROMÂNCE*, MARIA SOUDAYEVA, 1979

12. INGRID VOGEL, *ROMÂNCE*, MARIA SOUDAYEVA, 1979

13. TO DIE UNFETTERED, *FANTASIA*, INFERNUS IOHANNES, 1980

14. THE COLD PRINCES, *SHAGGÂS*, MARIA ECHENGUYEN, 1980

15. TOMORROW, THE FLAMES, *ROMÂNCE*, MARIA SCHRAG, 1980

16. A SUNDAY IN ORBISE, *ROMÂNCE*, MARIA SOUDAYEVA, 1980

17. THE ANATHEMAS, *ROMÂNCE*, JULIO STERNHAGEN, 1981

18. DRIFT, *ROMÂNCE*, IAKOUB KHADJBAKIRO, 1981

19. DISCOURSE ON SPIDER MITES, *FANTASIA*, WERNIERI, 1981

20. MOYOCOATZIN, *FANTASIA*, MARIA SCHRAG, 1981

21. To Embrace Again, *romånce*, Maria Schrag, 1981
22. Kromwell Calls Tassili, *romånce*, Wolfgang Gardel, 1981
23. The Brick Walls, *romånce*, Jean Wolguelam, 1981
24. The Centipedes, *fantasia*, Maria Echenguyen, 1981
25. One Bright Morning, *romånce*, Irena Echenguyen, 1981
26. Warriors in the Rain, *romånce*, Wolfgang Gardel, 1981
27. Schlumm Calls Tassili, *romånce*, Wolfgang Gardel, 1982
28. The Beheaded Crocodile, *fantasia*, Maria Samarkande, 1982
29. Façade Restoration, *interjoists*, Khrili Gompo, 1982
30. Bloom's Mistake, *romånce*, Iakoub Khadjbakiro, 1982
31. Useless Weather Afterward, *interjoists*, Maria Samarkande, 1983
32. A Massacre Unlike the Others, *romånce*, Iakoub Khadjbakiro, 1983
33. Night in the Hand, *interjoists*, Maria Schnittke, 1983
34. The Earthen Faces, *romånce*, Maria Schnittke, 1983
35. Ytchordo's Love, *romånce*, Maria Samarkande, 1984
36. Crime #5, *romånce*, Khrili Gompo, 1984
37. A Doll in the Void, *romånce*, attributed to Maria Samarkande, 1984
38. An Old Rebirth, *interjoists*, Zeev Retzmayer, 1984
39. Distress on Board, *romånce*, Rita Retzmayer, 1984
40. A Recipe for Not Rotting, *interjoists*, Maria Schnittke, 1984

41. Ingrid Calls Orbise, *romance*, Lilith Schwack, 1984

42. The Price of Excellence, *lesson*, Rita Retzmayer, 1984

43. The Weapon Lodge, *interjoists*, Khrili Gompo, 1984

44. Comparative Biography of Jorian Murgrave, *romance*, attributed to Iakoub Khadjbakiro, 1985

45. Gloria Vancouver, *romance*, Istvan Breughel, 1985

46. Mooring Procedures, *fantasia*, Maria Schnittke, 1985

47. Treatise on Proletarian Mechanics, *romance*, Maria Schnittke, 1985

48. Adoration with Marionettes and Chamber Orchestra, *romance*, Rita Retzmayer, 1985

49. Blood Sisters, *romance*, attributed to Irena Soledad, 1985

50. When the Mouth Shudders, *romance*, Wernieri, 1985

51. The Solitude of the Suckerfish in the Fry-Pan, *interjoists*, Wernieri, 1985

52. Waterproof Dictionary, *romance*, Ralf Thielmann, 1985

53. A Clown Misses the Call, *romance*, Monika Santander, 1985

54. A Boat from Nowhere, *romance*, attributed to Wernieri, 1986

55. The Hero Hong and No One Else, *romance*, Verena Nordstrand, 1986

56. Dura Nox, Sed Nox, *romance*, attributed to Infernus Iohannes, 1986

57. Ritual of Contempt, *romance*, attributed to Julio Sternhagen, 1986

75. MONGOLIAN TRADITION, *ROMÂNCE*, YANN ZHANG, 1989

76. WORLD WAR THREE, *FANTASIA*, IRENA SOLEDAD, 1989

77. IGOR EUWE CALLS IGOR EUWE, *ROMÂNCE*, JEAN VLASSENKO, 1989

78. THE PALE FACES, *ROMÂNCE*, IRENA SOLEDAD, 1989

79. FOOLS BEFORE THE FENCE, *ROMÂNCE*, VASSILISSA LUKASZC-ZYK, 1989

80. THEATER OF HARROWING REVISION, *INTERJOISTS*, YANN ZHANG, 1990

81. EUWE CALLS TASSILI, *ROMÂNCE*, ATTRIBUTED TO IRENA SOLEDAD, 1990

82. VIXEN LAKE, *ROMÂNCE*, VASSILISSA LUKASZCZYK, 1990

83. LAST NIGHT BEFORE THE GREAT SLEEP, *ROMÂNCE*, GIUSEPPE CAMPANINI, 1990

84. SWIMMING LESSONS WITH CARP, *ROMÂNCE*, KYNTHIA BEDO-BUL, 1990

85. THE MULTIPLICATION OF CELLS, *INTERJOISTS*, ATTRIBUTED TO JEAN VLASSENKO, 1990

86. LISBON, LAST EDGE, *ROMÂNCE*, ATTRIBUTED TO VASSILISSA LUKASZCZYK, 1990

87. TASSILI CALLS FRAJELMAN, *ROMÂNCE*, ATTRIBUTED TO GIO-VAN BARTOK, 1990

88. THE TRUTH ABOUT THE SCARLATTI CASE, *ROMÂNCE*, GIO-VAN BARTOK, 1990

89. BROKEN HOPES COAST, *ROMÂNCE*, KYNTHIA BEDOBUL, 1991

90. A FLAG UNDER THE MUD, *ROMÂNCE*, YANN ZHANG, 1991

91. ALTO SOLO, *ROMÂNCE*, ATTRIBUTED TO JEAN VLASSENKO, 1991

92. THE ORCAS, *INTERJOISTS*, ANITA NEGRINI, 1991

93. FOR BETTER ACCOUNTABILITY OF DISINFORMATION, *LESSON*, GIOVAN BARTOK, 1991

94. THE DISMISSED CASE, *ROMÂNCE*, ANITA NEGRINI, 1991

95. THOSE WHO SPARKLE, *ROMÂNCE*, ATTRIBUTED TO ANITA NEGRINI, 1991

96. THE MUD, *ROMÂNCE*, ATTRIBUTED TO ANITA NEGRINI, 1991

97. ON THE SURFACE OF THE DEAD, *ROMÂNCE*, ATTRIBUTED TO DOROTHEA RETSCH, 1991

98. LETTER TO THE MONK OF WAR, *SHAGGÅS*, ATTRIBUTED TO RALF THIELMANN, 1991

99. THE KARAKASSIAN FOUNDATION, *ROMÂNCE*, ATTRIBUTED TO DOROTHEA RETSCH, 1991

100. ONE OF KHRILI GOMPO'S ADOLESCENT MEMORIES, *ROMÂNCE*, KYNTHIA BEDOBUL, 1992

101. MURDER IN BASE FOUR, *ROMÂNCE*, ANONYMOUS COLLECTIVE, 1992

102. VISIT TO THE ABYSS, *ROMÂNCE*, YASAR TARCHALSKI, 1992

103. A HERO AWAKES, *INTERJOISTS*, KYNTHIA BEDOBUL, 1992

104. DUST ON THE RIVER, *ROMÂNCE*, YASAR TARCHALSKI, 1992

105. DAYDREAM'S DREAM, *SHAGGÅS*, ANONYMOUS COLLECTIVE, 1992

106. A STARRY-EYED REPEAT OFFENDER, *ROMÂNCE*, ANONYMOUS COLLECTIVE, 1992

107. THE SCAR HORIZON, *ROMÂNCE*, YASAR TARCHALSKI, 1992

108. THE VISIONARY OF VICTORIA HARBOUR, *ROMÂNCE*, ATTRIBUTED TO MARIA KWOLL, 1992

109. ORBISE HERE, PLEASE RESPOND, *ROMÂNCE*, TÜRKAN MARACHVILI, 1992

110. THE ATTYLA STYLE, *LESSON*, JOHN WALLINGER, 1992

111. ELEVEN SHAGGÅS, *SHAGGÅS*, ARAM PETROKIAN, 1993

112. THE MELODY OF HAPPINESS, *SHAGGÅS*, ARAM PETROKIAN, 1993

113. PLANET FOR AN EMPTY MAN, *ROMÂNCE*, YASAR TARCHAL-SKI, 1993

114. SEVEN SHAGGÅS, *SHAGGÅS*, ARAM PETROKIAN, 1993

115. PETITION TO THE BENEVOLENT ONE #8, *INTERJOISTS*, ATTRIBUTED TO GIUSEPPE CAMPANINI, 1993

116. THE BRÈGNE TEACHER, *ROMÂNCE*, JOHN WALLINGER, 1993

117. CORRECTIVE TO THE INSURRECTIONARY PROGRAM #3, *ROMÂNCE*, JOHN WALLINGER, 1993

118. THE RED DWARFS' SONG, *ROMÂNCE*, YASAR TARCHALSKI, 1993

119. THE SOPHIE GIRONDE AFFAIR, *ROMÂNCE*, ATTRIBUTED TO DOROTHEA RETSCH, 1993

120. GOLD CALLS TASSILI, *ROMÂNCE*, GIOVAN BARTOK, 1993

121. ÉLIANE'S MEMOIRS, *LYRICAL NARRACTS*, ANONYMOUS COLLECTIVE, 1993

122. FIRE IN A CHINESE CEMETERY, *ROMÂNCE*, BARBARA HEIER, 1993

123. BACKDROP, *ROMÂNCE*, BARBARA HEIER, 1993

124. HOLD-UP, *ROMÂNCE*, PETRA KIM, 1993

125. CHARIVARI WITH THE INUITS, *ROMÂNCE*, ASTRID KOENIG, 1993

126. SHOT OF FIREDAMP, *ROMÂNCE*, ATTRIBUTED TO GIOVAN BARTOK, 1993

127. BOATS, *LYRICAL NARRACTS*, BARBARA HEIER, 1994

128. AUTUMN MALAISE, *ROMÅNCE*, ASTRID KOENIG, 1994

129. THE GRAY SAND, *INTERJOISTS*, PETRA KIM, 1994

130. NAMING THE JUNGLE, *ROMÅNCE*, ATTRIBUTED TO YASAR TARCHALSKI, 1994

131. BURGLARY IN ULAN BATOR, *ROMÅNCE*, BARBARA HEIER, 1994

132. A TWO-SPEED PRISON, *LESSON*, ATTRIBUTED TO BARBARA HEIER, 1994

133. END OF FAKIRISM, *INTERJOISTS*, ASTRID KOENIG, 1994

134. DISILLUSION EXPRESS, *INTERJOISTS*, YASAR TARCHALSKI, 1994

135. THE MASTIFFS, *ROMÅNCE*, YASAR TARCHALSKI, 1994

136. LEELA IN THE CITIES, *ROMÅNCE*, HUGO MALTER, 1994

137. LETTERS FOR LAGASH, *ROMÅNCE*, MATTHIAS BACH, 1994

138. APPENDIX, *LESSON*, ANONYMOUS, 1994

139. THE VOID FOR EVERYONE IN 49 LESSONS, *INTERJOISTS*, ANONYMOUS COLLECTIVE, 1994

140. SKIFF PORTSIDE, *ROMÅNCE*, MATTHIAS BACH, 1994

141. STATEMENT IN FAVOR OF EXTREMELY EXPLOSIVE PYRO-DYNAMITE, *LESSON*, HUGO MALTER, 1994

142. THE AUROCH IS A FALLEN BIRD, *ROMÅNCE*, ATTRIBUTED TO PETRA KIM, 1994

143. A ROSEWOOD UTERUS, *ROMÅNCE*, ATTRIBUTED TO MATTHIAS BACH, 1994

144. DEATH TO RATS, *ROMÅNCE*, ATTRIBUTED TO MATTHIAS BACH, 1994

145. BRAINTEASER UNDER A SKULL, *ROMÅNCE*, ATTRIBUTED TO MATTHIAS BACH, 1994

146. THE LAST ROW, ROMÂNCE, ANONYMOUS, 1994

147. SQUARING THE EGG, INTERJOISTS, ANONYMOUS, 1995

148. TROOP TRANSPORT, ROMÂNCE, ANONYMOUS, 1995

149. LOCKING, ROMÂNCE, HUGO MALTER, 1995

150. THE SUBLIME DOOR, ROMÂNCE, HUGO MALTER, 1995

151. WE THE ROOTS, LESSON, ASTRID KOENIG, 1995

152. BORSHOYED CALLS TASSILI, ROMÂNCE, YASAR TARCHALSKI, 1995

153. FIGHTING ALONE, ROMÂNCE, IVO MARCONI, 1995

154. STRONG BREEZE, ROMÂNCE, MARIA GABRIELA THIELMANN, 1995

155. A ROBIN WADES IN, ROMÂNCE, IVO MARCONI, 1995

156. TOMORROW WILL HAVE BEEN A LOVELY SUNDAY, INTERJOISTS, ANONYMOUS, 1995

157. WOMAN WITH SANSKRIT SMILE, ROMÂNCE, ANONYMOUS, 1995

158. THE COCAMBOS, ROMÂNCE, MARIA GABRIELA THIELMANN, 1995

159. A BARN OWL, ROMÂNCE, IVO MARCONI, 1995

160. FIRST MIRE, LYRICAL NARRACTS, IVO MARCONI, 1995

161. A SHAGGÅ FOR TOTHORI, ROMÂNCE, IRINA KOBAYASHI, 1995

162. ON THE CORRECT USE OF THE GUILLOTINE AT SUNSET, INTERJOISTS, IRINA KOBAYASHI, 1995

163. THE CLAY LADY, ROMÂNCE, ATTRIBUTED TO JEAN WOLGUELAM, 1995

164. PLAGIARISM, LESSON, ANONYMOUS COLLECTIVE, 1995

165. THE DORDJI NEBULA, ROMÂNCE, JEAN MALAYSI, 1995

166. SIBYLLE AND THE JUCAPIRAS, ROMÂNCE, ATTRIBUTED TO JEAN MALAYSI, 1995

167. ON-TIME BIRTH, *POETIC NARRACTS*, ATTRIBUTED TO JEAN MALAYSI, 1995

168. THE WALTZ UNDER THE LIME TREES, *ROMÂNCE*, IRINA KOBAYASHI, 1996

169. THE MASTER OF THE PRISON REGISTERS, *LESSON*, IVO MARCONI, 1996

170. SHORT TETRALOGY FOR STAMMERERS, *POETIC NARRACTS*, WILLIAM LETHBRIDGE, 1996

171. FOR THE ANNIVERSARY OF ANITA NEGRINI'S DEATH, *LESSON*, ATTRIBUTED TO IVO MARCONI, 1996

172. EQUINE BUTCHERY, *ROMÂNCE*, DIMITRI REDDECLIFF, 1996

173. A BLUEBIRD'S CRY, *ROMÂNCE*, PABLO OSTIATEGUI, 1996

174. THE NAVE PROOF, *SHAGGÂS*, IRINA KOBAYASHI, 1996

175. THE VILE METAL, *INTERJOISTS*, WILLIAM LETHBRIDGE, 1996

176. SLAG DOESN'T PAY, *ROMÂNCE*, LEONOR OSTIATEGUI, 1996

177. FROM OUR COLLABORATOR IN URUK, *ROMÂNCE*, LEONOR OSTIATEGUI, 1996

178. THE BANK OF TEARS, *ROMÂNCE*, RAÏA OSSORGUINA, 1996

179. A MARTIN AS FAR AS THE EYE CAN SEE, *INTERJOISTS*, DIMITRI REDDECLIFF, 1996

180. THE TELEGRAPH LADIES, *ROMÂNCE*, RAÏA OSSORGUINA, 1996

181. MY HERMETIC TESTAMENT, *POETIC NARRACTS*, RITA HOO, 1996

182. THE INNER HARBOUR, *ROMÂNCE*, ATTRIBUTED TO RITA HOO, 1996

183. THE DEATHS ONE CROSSES BEFORE LOVE, *SHAGGÂS*, ELLEN DAWKES, 1996

184. An Udmurt King, ROMÂNCE, Jean Khorassan, 1996
185. Toghtaga Özbeg Calls Tassili, ROMÂNCE, Jean Khorassan, 1996
186. Out of the Blue, INTERJOISTS, Yasar Tarchalski, 1996
187. Apple Scabs and Company, LESSON, Aidan Sherrad, 1996
188. The Golfox House, ROMÂNCE, Türkan Marachvili, 1996
189. Spotted Wheat, ROMÂNCE, Türkan Marachvili, 1996
190. The Nightingale's Mathematics, ROMÂNCE, ATTRIBUTED TO Verena Nordstrand, 1996
191. A Cure for Shibboleth, ROMÂNCE, William Lethbridge, 1996
192. Waterway, ROMÂNCE, Dimitri Reddecliff, 1996
193. A Dull Idiot, ROMÂNCE, Irina Kobayashi, 1996
194. Alcina, ROMÂNCE, Vassilissa Lukaszczyk, 1996
195. Dangerous Verbiage, INTERJOISTS, Irina Kobayashi, 1996
196. Low Waters, Waters Very Low, ROMÂNCE, ATTRIBUTED TO Irina Kobayashi, 1996
197. Firepath, INTERJOISTS, ANONYMOUS, 1996
198. Ali-Baba and the Forty Heaves, INTERJOISTS, ANONYMOUS, 1996
199. Homage to Vladimir "Che" Bronstein, LESSON, Vassilissa Lukaszczyk collective, 1996
200. Comparative Biography of Catfish, ROMÂNCE, Raïa Ossorguina, 1996
201. Lacquers, POETIC NARRACTS, Pablo Ostiategui, 1996
202. Prelude to Devastation, ROMÂNCE, Pablo Ostiategui, 1996

218. LOCKOUT, *LESSON*, VERENA NORDSTRAND FRACTION, 1997

219. THE CONDUIT, *ROMÅNCE*, YASAR TARCHALSKI, 1998

220. A HEN AT BLOUDY-MONGO'S, *ROMÅNCE*, JEAN KHORASSAN, 1998

221. THE FIRST CLOUD, *FANTASIA*, LILITH SCHWACK COLLECTIVE, 1998

222. A LONG-NOSE WEDDING, *ROMÅNCE*, TÜRKAN MARACHVILI, 1998

223. KNOCK AND YOU WILL BE RECEIVED, *ROMÅNCE*, ELIA FINCKE, 1998

224. EQUATION WITH THREE UNKNOWNS, *ROMÅNCE*, JEAN KHORASSAN, 1998

225. CELESTIAL MECHANICS, *ROMÅNCE*, ANONYMOUS, 1998

226. VIEW OVER THE OSSUARY, *ROMÅNCE*, ATTRIBUTED TO JEAN KHORASSAN, 1998

227. SECOND SEARCH, *INTERJOISTS*, RAÏA OSSORGUINA, 1998

228. THE GREAT BROOD, *ROMÅNCE*, ANONYMOUS COLLECTIVE, 1998

229. CRISIS AT THE TONG FONG HOTEL, *ROMÅNCE*, TÜRKAN MARACHVILI, 1999

230. MISTER MARCO, *ROMÅNCE*, ATTRIBUTED TO RAÏA OSSORGUINA, 1999

231. ALREADY MIDNIGHT, *ROMÅNCE*, JEAN KHORASSAN COLLECTIVE, 1999

232. THE LION HOBBYIST, *ROMÅNCE*, VERENA NORDSTRAND FRACTION, 1999

233. A NOTCH ON THE LEFT EYE, *ROMÅNCE*, ELIA FINCKE, 1999

234. RUMORS AND ANTS AND ANKLEBONES, *POETIC NARRACTS*, ELIA FINCKE, 1999

235. THE FALSE TEETH, *INTERJOISTS*, ELLEN DAWKES, 1999

236. AUTOPSY OF A KOREAN WOMAN, *ROMÅNCE*, PETRA KIM COLLECTIVE, 1999

237. PIANO, *ROMÅNCE*, ANONYMOUS, 1999

238. DOPPELGÄNGERS IN THE TUNNEL, *ROMÅNCE*, ERDOGAN MAYAYO, 1999

239. CONVERSATION WITH A SHE-WOLF, *FANTASIA*, MARINA PEEK, 1999

240. A MITE NAMED LOUIS, *FANTASIA*, OLEG DAMTEW, 1999

241. MARTIAL LIZARD, *LESSON*, OLEG DAMTEW, 1999

242. SO NO ONE GETS OUT, *LESSON*, ELIA FINCKE, 2000

243. THE ASSAULTS AGAINST THE MOON, *ROMÅNCE*, ATTRIBUTED TO LUTZ BASSMANN, 2000

244. STYX, *ROMÅNCE*, ANONYMOUS, 2000

245. WHY I KILLED SYLVIO POMPONI, *ROMÅNCE*, MARINA PEEK COMMANDO UNIT, 2001

246. ENUCLEATE HERE, *ROMÅNCE*, ATTRIBUTED TO YASAR TARCHALSKI, 2001

247. A DROP OF MERCURY, *INTERJOISTS*, MARIO HINZ, 2001

248. THE GREAT LADDER, *ROMÅNCE*, MONIKA DOMROWSKI, 2001

249. RESENTMENT, *LESSON*, ELLI KRONAUER, 2001

250. ON THE FORBIDDANCE OF DWARF TOSSING AND ITS CONSEQUENCES ON THE ENVIRONMENT, *ROMÅNCE*, HANS-JÜRGEN PIZARRO, 2001

304. THE ARREST OF THE GREAT MIMILLE, *ROMÅNCE*, MANUELA DRAEGER, 2007

305. HOSPICE EXCHANGE, *ROMÅNCE*, MARIA SAUERBAUM, 2007

306. THE HUNT FOR THE MOCKING PLATONOV, *INTERJOISTS*, REBECCA WOLFF, 2008

307. THE HOUR OF THE ELEVEN O'CLOCK SOUP, *ROMÅNCE*, MARIA CLEMENTI COMPANY, 2008

308. BREAKTHROUGH, *LESSON*, WERNIERI CELL, 2008

309. GRIS-GRIS, *POETIC NARRACTS*, MARIA SAUERBAUM, 2008

310. ALARM SIGNAL FOR HARD-OF-HEARING DROMEDARIES, *ROMÅNCE*, MARIO HINZ, 2008

311. AFTER ALL, *INTERJOISTS*, MANUELA DRAEGER, 2008

312. A PLUSH CLOWN, *ROMÅNCE*, LUTZ BASSMANN, 2008

313. THE PERFECT DUST, *INTERJOISTS*, LUTZ BASSMANN, 2009

314. NOD TO VIRGINIA WOOLF, *LESSON*, ANONYMOUS, 2009

315. DEPARTURE TO DETACHMENT, *ROMÅNCE*, MANUELA DRAEGER, 2009

316. A HILARIOUS VARIETY OF ATOMIC WARS, *FANTASIA*, LUTZ BASSMANN, 2009

317. WERNIERI CALLS TASSILI, *ROMÅNCE*, MARIA SAUERBAUM, 2009

318. THE PHARAOHS BEFORE THE DOOR, *ROMÅNCE*, MARIO HINZ, 2009

319. THE MANTIS, *ROMÅNCE*, LUTZ BASSMANN, 2011

320. BALBUTIAR IV'S FLING, *INTERJOISTS*, MANUELA DRAEGER CELL, 2011

321. NIVÔSE, YEAR THOUSAND, *SHAGGÅS*, MARIO HINZ CELL, 2012

322. CONCERNING MY SO-CALLED GODDAUGHTER, *ROMÅNCE*, ANONYMOUS, NO DATE (N.D.)

323. ABOUT-FACE VANDALS, *ROMÅNCE*, ANONYMOUS, N.D.

324. AN ESSENTIAL ELEMENT OF DISASTER, *ROMÅNCE*, ATTRIBUTED TO THE MARIA SCHRAG CELL, N.D.

325. THE MAGICIANS, *ROMÅNCE*, ANONYMOUS, N.D.

326. TO KNOW HOW TO ROT, TO KNOW HOW NOT TO ROT, *POETIC NARRACTS*, LUTZ BASSMANN, N.D.

327. IN THE TORPEDO'S WAKE, *INTERJOISTS*, ATTRIBUTED TO THE MARIO HINZ CELL, N.D.

328. A LAMA ON THE EAST COAST, *ROMÅNCE*, ATTRIBUTED TO THE MANUELA DRAEGER FRACTION, N.D.

329. RANTING AT ARTHROPODS, *ROMÅNCE*, ANONYMOUS, N.D.

330. THE COUNTRY WHERE MARIA SCHRAG WAS BORN, *ROMÅNCE*, ANONYMOUS, N.D.

331. ATTEMPT TO REACTIVATE AN OLD MOLE MACHINE, *ROMÅNCE*, ANONYMOUS, N.D.

332. THE GIRL FROM THE VASSORINE OBLEGAT, *ROMÅNCE*, ANONYMOUS, N.D.

333. THE DECLINE OF THE STATE DURING FEVERS, *ROMÅNCE*, LUTZ BASSMANN, N.D.

334. METAMORPHOSIS OF A SACRED COW, *ROMÅNCE*, ANONYMOUS, N.D.

335. POSTHUMOUS WRATH, *POETIC NARRACTS*, ANONYMOUS, N.D.

336. THE POISONOUS MUSHROOMS, *ROMÅNCE*, ANONYMOUS, N.D.

337. STRUCTURE OF DECONSTRUCTED OBSCURITY, *SHAGGÅS*, ANONYMOUS, N.D.

338. PETROGRAD CALLS TASSILI, *ROMÅNCE*, ANONYMOUS, N.D.

339. ONE THOUSAND NINE HUNDRED SEVENTY-SEVEN YEARS BEFORE THE WORLD REVOLUTION, *ROMÅNCE*, LUTZ BASSMANN, N.D.

340. LAST GASP AND OTHER DREAM FRAGMENTS, *POETIC NARRACTS*, LUTZ BASSMANN, N.D.

341. WALK THROUGH CHILDHOOD, *POETIC NARRACTS*, LUTZ BASSMANN, N.D.

342. BASSMANN CALLS TASSILI, *FANTASIA*, ANONYMOUS, N.D.

343. RETURN TO THE TAR, *ROMÅNCE*, ATTRIBUTED TO LUTZ BASSMANN, N.D.

Antoine Volodine is the primary pseudonym of a French writer who has published 20 books under this name, several of which are available in English translation, including *Minor Angels*, *Naming the Jungle*, and *Writers*. He also publishes under the names Lutz Bassmann (*We Monks & Soldiers*) and Manuela Draeger (*In the Time of the Blue Ball*). Most of his works take place in a post-apocalyptic world where members of the "post-exoticism" writing movement have all been arrested as subversive elements. Together, these works constitute one of the most inventive, ambitious projects of contemporary writing.

J. T. Mahany is a graduate of the masters program in literary translation at the University of Rochester and is currently enrolled in the MFA program at the University of Arkansas. He is in the process of translating several more books by the enigmatic and intriguing French author, Antoine Volodine.

Open Letter—the University of Rochester's nonprofit, literary translation press—is one of only a handful of publishing houses dedicated to increasing access to world literature for English readers. Publishing ten titles in translation each year, Open Letter searches for works that are extraordinary and influential, works that we hope will become the classics of tomorrow.

Making world literature available in English is crucial to opening our cultural borders, and its availability plays a vital role in maintaining a healthy and vibrant book culture. Open Letter strives to cultivate an audience for these works by helping readers discover imaginative, stunning works of fiction and poetry, and by creating a constellation of international writing that is engaging, stimulating, and enduring.

Current and forthcoming titles from Open Letter include works from Argentina, Bulgaria, China, Greece, Iceland, Israel, Latvia, Poland, South Africa, and many other countries.

www.openletterbooks.org